———————— ★ ————————

I tried to scream.

Mistake.

Suddenly I was as tall as the top shelf and flying. I landed on my hip and shoulder, too stunned to do anything but watch as he dumped the contents of my purse into a brown paper bag, which he then stuffed into one of his inside pockets. He watched me watching him, with no expression whatever. Taking all the time in the world, he felt around the bottom of the now-empty bag with one finger. Obviously, he wanted more than money. Why wasn't someone coming? Didn't anyone hear me fall? Finding nothing more, he tossed the empty bag on my stomach. Too bulky to take with him, I guessed.

"We told you to back off, lady," he snarled, landing a kick on my thigh. "Next time it's for keeps." Now I did scream, and hard. He backed around another shelf and was gone.

———————— ★ ————————

"This capable novel benefits from its refreshing look at the world of small-plane flying."

—*Booklist*

Forthcoming from Worldwide Mystery by
JACKIE LEWIN

DEATH FLIES ON FINAL

MURDER FLIES LEFT SEAT

JACKIE LEWIN

WORLDWIDE.

TORONTO • NEW YORK • LONDON
AMSTERDAM • PARIS • SYDNEY • HAMBURG
STOCKHOLM • ATHENS • TOKYO • MILAN
MADRID • WARSAW • BUDAPEST • AUCKLAND

MURDER FLIES LEFT SEAT

A Worldwide Mystery/August 2000

First published by Thomas Bouregy & Company, Inc.

ISBN 0-373-26357-0

Acknowledgments

This book would have been quite impossible without the help of people who have forgotten more about planes than with luck I'll ever know: Rodney Getty, Tony Charleston and my intrepid husband, Ed Lewin. For scientific aid and abettance, I'm indebted particularly to Judy and Kedar Prasad and Tim Johnson, John and Becky Lewin, Jerry Morse and the totally amazing librarians at the Denver Public Library. Writers Sandy Lamb and Blanche Boshinski read, edited and advised, as did a particularly literate lawyer, one Cynthia Lewin. Lowell helped too. To all, I am deeply grateful.

ONE

THE PIPER WAS GONE. Splitsville. Vanished from its hangar. I couldn't believe my good fortune.

Less than half an hour ago, driving to the airport, I'd been in my usual funk. We were in for another of those weekends spent bumping our way to odd-ball destinations, sites known primarily, to my husband at least, for having places to land. Admittedly, some of these adventures had been fun, once we arrived. Note: Once we arrived.

Obviously, flying in small planes is just not my thing. The cabins are more cramped than a dental chair (and about as inviting), the front window so high, the only time I can see where we're going is when we're headed straight down—which is when I don't want to look. And then there's the turbulence.

The best pilot in the world can't keep the planes in this part of the west from bouncing. The mountains do their damage to all the air currents in the vicinity and planes just fall through the troughs. I can handle it in those gigantic flying movie palaces, but in Albert's Turbo Arrow, turbulence feels like trouble. When it starts, I grip the door strap with one hand, wrap my left arm around the other seat (the one with him in it), and ride out the nastiness with every muscle clenched.

So why do I keep doing it? Because Albert loves it, that's why, and I'm a good person. And actually, there aren't that many parts of his life beyond our family that I can share. So that's a plus. Still, I could use some help handling this, like maybe a nice, reliable twelve-step program. *"Hello,"* I'd say, standing bravely in front of the crowd. *"My name is Grace Spence Beckmann and I am a wimp."*

So there we were, driving to the general aviation airport that housed our private plane, and naturally I was thinking black thoughts. Unhappy as I was, though, it was hard not to notice that the day itself was gorgeous. The route wound through low foothills crested with the flat light of morning. Wild October grasses, their scent overripe, were just beginning to lose color on both sides of the road, but not the interest of several horses enjoying the fall air. The sky was clear, the mountains freshly snow-fringed in the distance. The few flags we passed along the way hung limply on their poles, but none of that serenity meant a thing. Hidden in the deceptively calm ether, in that unsullied blue, was doubtless enough turbulence to smack a small plane all over the sky.

Albert was, not atypically, splashing in his own brain waves. He slowed for a barn swallow that had landed on the road. "Ever wonder," he mused, waiting till the bird had flown off, "why people always screw things up? I mean, why don't they ever screw things down?"

Only my husband could make a perfectly ordinary

expression sound academic. "Hush," I grumbled. "I need to concentrate."

"On?"

"Deep breathing and alpha rhythms."

He was saved from struggling for a clever retort by the turnoff to the airport coming up on our left. Our bright red, low-nosed Aurora veered in, sniffing the way. Past corporate offices and FBOs, we drove beyond the tower with its scanning windows and almost to the end of the road where the hangar we shared with a few other owners squatted. It looked so innocent. We parked against the side wall away from the street and removed such luggage as we had, a couple of small duffels and a backpack for possible hiking. Since our plan was for only a long weekend spent largely in the lonelier stretches of Wyoming, the area around Devil's Tower, we'd dutifully packed light. That was never a problem for me. I love clothes like I love Pipers.

Albert busied himself checking his flight bag, keys, wallet, and whatever. "I do wish you enjoyed this more," he said, serious for once. "You're missing the thrill."

"When we survive, I'm thrilled."

"It's really time you learned to fly yourself. It would be so much more fun for you."

I'd heard that one before, of course. No way was I going to take flying lessons. He didn't need any more encouragement than he already had.

Now that we were actually at the hangar, all my warning systems were on red alert. "I'm sure you know enough for both of us," I muttered, realizing

I'd need to stop at the rest room before takeoff. Nerves always had that effect on me. Where other people dreamed they were running wildly around their school trying to find the place where a test was being given, I used to dream I couldn't find the girls' room. In the old days when I was just starting out as a magazine writer, green and uncertain with the ink barely dry on my English degree, I'd had trouble getting through an important interview without having to take a break.

Albert wouldn't dignify my last dig with a response. We entered the hangar by the small side door and found it empty of planes, the gray-painted cement floor clean and gleaming. Jack Potts, the mechanic and, for the moment, general factotum, was on the far side attacking the corner with a large broom. He looked up at us with what read as surprise.

Albert didn't appear to notice. "Morning," he called, full of good cheer. He dropped the duffel bags and spread our coats carefully on top. "Looks like all the planes are out today."

Jack Potts returned the broom to its position against the back wall and walked over, wiping his hands on wrinkled gray cords. Obviously puzzled, his forehead creased where the thin hair was receding. He was a small man in every particular, short, lithe, and somehow dainty in his movements. His slim fingers were at home among the intricate workings of engines and other esoterica. Having found his natural bent shortly after high school, he'd settled into his chosen career and never again thought of another line of work.

"Yeah, they're out. Yours, too, Dr. B. I thought there must have been a change of plans."

Albert glanced out the wide open doors to the ramp. A few small planes were tied down nearby. A collector's Stearman and a Citabria waited in the distance. None of the planes were ours. He turned to Potts. "Of course I was planning to use it. I called two hours ago and told the line guys to take it out and get it ready. Any idea where it is?"

"A pretty good idea," said the mechanic. "Up there." He pointed toward the cloudless sky.

Albert looked at me nonplussed, then back at Potts. "Well, what...? Who...? What the heck is going on? We were planning to take the plane for the weekend. Parker knew we were using it. He was okay with that. Did he take it out after all?"

Potts paused. "Not exactly, no."

Parker LeMay was our co-owner and, until then, we'd never had a problem sharing the plane. The men had chosen their midlife toy together, agreed never to put it in a rental pool for students, and enjoyed a remarkably polite relationship, cordial if not close. Financially, the partnership was problem-free. The LeMays seemed able to afford the luxury of owning a gadget that occasionally swilled money, never balking at the bills for annual inspections or the repairs they turned up. It was almost inconceivable that Parker would deliberately take the plane when we had reserved it. Albert was clearly blown away by the idea. Honoring his distress, I didn't say a word. Only thought it. *There is a God.*

"Well, if it wasn't Parker, then who took it"— he pointed— "up there?"

Potts shrugged. "It was his wife." He used the moment it took for Albert to digest this information to dodge into the tiny bathroom in the corner. Immediately, I heard water running. He returned shortly, wiping his hands on paper towels. For a man who spent his working life covered with engine oil, his hands and nails were spotless. He smelled of strong soap.

"Jann took the plane?" Albert couldn't quite come to grips with this outrage. "How could anyone let her take the plane? I was the one who called to take it out."

"Sorry, Dr. B. Don't know what to say. I told her I thought you two were flying today. She said she just had to check something out in the plane. Or she'd left something there. I can't remember. Anyway, I didn't know she was going to take off."

Albert rubbed his eyes slowly. He was having big trouble with this. "Well, um, how did she look? How was she dressed? Did she have a suitcase or something with her?"

Jack Potts crossed his arms, body language for "Wait a minute, this isn't my fault." "Hey, I was just as surprised as you are. But to answer your questions, she looked a little funny. Kinda shaky. But, well, you know, otherwise she always looks real classy." Realizing Albert wanted more, he went on. "She had on something silky, sort of silky and light brown. A pantsuit, I guess. Tight.'' He smiled at the recollection. ''And she didn't have anything with her but a purse. I mean, no flight stuff. That's why it never occurred to me that she was going to fly. She did have a package with her, though, I remember.''

''A package?''

''Small. Shorter than a loaf of bread. Wrapped in brown paper and tied up. From the way she was carrying it, it looked a little on the heavy side, but not so's she'd need me to help with it.''

Albert shook his head, staring out at the ramp as if to reconstruct the whole absurd scene. ''So then what happened?''

''She asked me to go back into the hangar to see if she left her plane key on the cabinet in the back. So I did, and I was almost there when I heard the propeller start up and she's moving. No preflight, no nothing. Didn't sump the tanks. I yelled at her, but she didn't hear me. I ran outside and watched, and seriously, I couldn't believe it. She didn't even do a run-up. Just taxied to the runway, stopped just long enough to look, and took off.''

''Curiouser and curiouser,'' muttered my man. Then, ''Maybe you just missed seeing the run-up.''

The mechanic didn't answer, but his look said don't bet the rent.

Albert picked up our duffels from the hangar floor, throwing one over his broad shoulder. ''I'm sure there's some explanation for all this,'' he said to no one in particular, ''but it's certainly screwing up our weekend.'' We left the hangar the way we came and walked back to the car in a semi-daze. "Maybe she just took it up for a couple of touch-and-goes," said Albert without conviction, slamming the trunk over our now useless bags. *And maybe,* I prayed, *she took it to Alaska.*

My relief at not having to fly was so palpable I was afraid it would show, so I stayed a step behind and tried not to grin. Admittedly, the relief was mixed with suspicion. A very odd story. Still, I could understand wanting to avoid all the preflight nonsense and just taking off. Men, not women, are the ritual-lovers, and flying is full of rituals. From what I'd heard from the tennis girls about Jann LeMay, she probably didn't have time or inclination for nonessentials in her life. However, I shared none of these thoughts. There are times in a marriage when the only sensible thing to say is nothing at all. When Albert decided we should walk to our own FBO to see if there was anything more to learn, I fell quietly in beside him.

When we fly, we much prefer getting off as early in the morning as we can, the skies being smoother before the day heats up. We'd been hurrying since our quick breakfast and found we couldn't slow the pace by much even though there was suddenly no rush whatever. We clipped along, at the same time feeling stalled, unfinished, like the apocryphal soprano who supposedly said when the opera was canceled, "You can't do this to me. I've already thrown up." We were moving fast, but not too fast to notice and greet some of the regulars who could usually be found around planes. Tony, one of Albert's former flying teachers, waved from a distance, yet another ambitious young man trying to accumulate hours in hopes of a career as an airline pilot. A charter operator eager to rent the Turbo Arrow started over but, perhaps seeing the expression on Albert's face, thought better of it. Only a few planes were left tied down on this perfect day and the poor things looked like they wanted to be adopted.

The brief glimpse of business-as-usual disappeared fast. The minute the automatic doors to our Fixed Base Operator swung open and we went in, we sensed trouble. Sally, the aging blond who usually manned the counter and knew everyone in the area, was standing inside the open door of the line shack that housed the scanner. Her blue knit pants hung flat in the back but stretched unpleasantly over a protruding abdomen. She always looked like the contents had shifted during shipping. Her expression seemed uncharacteristically tense. Seeing that it was us, she returned to her post at the desk where we were waiting. "Okay," she said accusingly. "Where's your plane?"

"What?"

"There's a problem," she said, tipping her head toward the device that monitored all the radio frequencies important to the running of the airport. "It sounds like maybe a plane is down. In fact, it sounds like it could be *your* plane that's down. Similar numbers. So if it's here somewhere, let us know now. Then we rethink this."

There's a funny electric buzz that goes through me during moments of sudden insight, particularly when the insight is ominous. Right now, I could have powered a halogen lamp. "It's ours," I said to Sally, unable to control the edge in my voice. "I'll bet anything it's ours."

"Now wait a minute." Albert gave me a husband look, the one that said *Receive, do not send.* "It's true our plane isn't here at the moment, but we know who has it. There's certainly no reason to believe she's crashed." I could see the next thought arc through his mind. "Though I guess there's some reason to believe she didn't follow procedure during her takeoff. But what makes you even suspect it's ours? That's ridiculous."

"You said 'she,' huh? Interesting. A Lear jet heard something. The pilot was about to call the tower when he heard a woman. She was trying to get the tower but it couldn't hear her. The Lear figures she was somewhere in the mountains since the signal was blocked. The jet could hear because it was still pretty high—about twenty-some thousand feet at that point. It was starting to come in."

"A woman?" My buzz was starting again.

"The Lear heard her give a Juliett. And maybe a 4 and a 6 and 7 or the reverse. Pretty close to your numbers." In the Alfa, Bravo, Charlie alphabet pilots use, the "J" is Juliett. Our plane's ID did indeed have some of those numbers followed by a J. I was just used to thinking of it as Sweet Juliet, and forget that second "t."

A few people who were in the FBO waiting room had wandered over, caught by the tone of our conversation. Albert ignored them, focusing totally on the woman in back of the desk. "What was she saying?"

"Well, shoot, I don't know exactly. It's, like, third-hand. Something like, " 'Help me. I can't handle the plane. Something's wrong with the controls. Nothing's working.'" She was getting into the drama. Her voice was mimicking panic.

"Anything else?"

"She wanted to come in."

"Anything else?"

"Yeah, maybe. The Lear pilot thought he heard one more thing but it wasn't absolutely clear. It's a miracle he heard her at all."

"And it was...?"

"Well, just that she seemed to start speaking, maybe, a foreign language. Or else she was babbling. Up till then, he'd been able to understand her. There was this crack and a scream. The Lear guy was really shook up. He called us right away. We've alerted the Civil Air Patrol. Also, it's possible there's been a satellite recording of an ELT in this vicinity. We're checking."

"Electronic Locator Transmitter," Albert explained quietly. Part of my passive rebellion is a refusal to learn all these initials. "Makes it possible to find a downed plane."

"Are you okay, Mrs. Beckmann? You look... well, not too good. Sorry, I guess I came on a little too strong here."

"That's all right, Sally. But we were planning to fly that plane up to Wyoming today, so naturally, if it is ours, I can't help wondering—"

Albert broke in before I could speculate further. "Nothing on radar, I suppose."

She shook her head. "Uh-uh. All the planes on radar are accounted for. She was probably flying too low. Plus, we checked with Flight Service. We don't think she filed a flight plan." She took a sip of something brown that had long since gone flat. "Say, what was that about not following procedure? With your plane, I mean. And who's in it, anyway?"

"Jann LeMay. And we heard she took off without a run-up."

"Oh, let me tell you." Her whoop attracted the attention of the manager, who was still in the line shack. He came out, a sturdy, clean-shaven man, rolling down the cuffs of his red sport shirt when he saw me. The lower arms were thick and sinewy. I was sorry to see them disappear. "Harley, I think we know who the nut case was."

He nodded at us and listened while Sally caught him up on our conversation. She turned back to us. "Close to an hour ago, some jerk took off without even contacting the tower for a by-your-leave. Lucky we weren't busy. Boy, the tower was furious. We were hearing them. 'Aircraft on Alfa taxiway, what is your intention?'" She raised her voice to act a part yet again. "'You do not have permission to be on the runway! Abort this takeoff immediately and return to the ramp.' You know how they sound. They were going to send the Blazer to intercept but it happened too fast."

Suddenly, I'd had enough. All the Sturm and

Drang was getting to me. Albert hung around the desk a while longer, but I wandered off. Outside the door to the ramp, people were beginning to cluster. A linesman was talking to what seemed to be a small group of private owners, gesturing as they moved toward the entrance. I could see Tony in conversation with a broker we knew, and everyone was heading for the FBO, the only place that offered somewhere to talk away from the wind that had started up on the field. Word of the emergency was clearly spreading from building to building along the runways. A few people were clutching handheld scanners, listening as they walked for any breaking news. Downed planes are like power outages or two-foot snowfalls. Shared Acts of God. Or man. I wondered into which category *Sweet Juliet* fell.

The TV in the carpeted lounge was blaring to an empty couch. I stopped for a minute to listen. There was no news bulletin, no deviation from the usual mindless local daytime features. No announcer was telling the story of a downed plane that, but for a quirk of fate, would have contained one Dr. and Mrs. Albert Beckmann on their way to a vacation weekend. No mention that the attractive, well-liked couple, pillars of the community, left twin sixteen-year-old sons, Paul and Spence, who were at present staying with friends. Announcers didn't happen to be saying that, but they could have been. Oh yes, they could have been.

TWO

ALBERT JOINED ME in the lounge and we headed silently through the hall toward a tiny lunchroom of sorts in the rear of the building. We needed a cup of coffee and a place to think our troubling thoughts. This was all too impossible, too coincidental. Just because Jann LeMay had more or less swiped our plane out from under us, that didn't mean she was the woman who had crashed. Not necessarily. And Jann was a terrific pilot. Well, pretty good anyway. Or was she? The fact was, we really didn't know either of the LeMays very well.

It had all started, with the LeMays that is, at one of those strange medical school quasi-parties where everyone stood around pretending that departmental money had paid for the catered munchies. Of course, everyone knew that the afternoon (usually) or evening (sometimes) was really being sponsored by one or another drug company doing its subliminal thing. Nothing heavy-handed, no obvious shilling. Just the presence of detail men smiling and playing host.

Albert had had his pilot's license for maybe a year, so that made the party probably four years ago, roughly. And my husband was obsessed. Flying, I used to remind him, was the only mistress he was going to be allowed, and he made the most of it. Besotted as he was, thoughts of the new passion intruded in every aspect of his life. He was, in those days, completely obnoxious. He couldn't refer to a letter of the alphabet without converting it to plane code. When he threatened Spence that he'd be grounded if he got a Foxtrot on his report card, both boys whooped. Of course, every nine became "niner," just in case someone confused it with a five, which no one ever did. Sporty's catalogs clogged the mailbox.

Then there were the times we flew commercially. Boy, I rued the day they allowed passengers to listen to the cockpit radio during flight. Earphones clasped to his head, Albert was in charge, banking, heading on final, choosing a runway. Gear down! Flaps! He was very happy and very audible. I burrowed into my book and tried to pretend the man next to me was the fault of the seating computer. His joy in this newfound game was almost total.

Until he began to want his own plane.

So there he was at this med school party, talking about you know what. Since he's head of Internal Medicine at the school, naturally the drug company men were making sure his needs were being well met. They probably wondered, as they hovered around nursing Scotch rocks, why he didn't just up and buy a plane. Any plane. His mother's name was not exactly unknown. Half the expensive designer sheets and towels in America carried the name of the family textile mills on those little slips of attached cloth. I mean, these were the kind of bed-and-bath luxuries they didn't sell at Wal-Mart. All those within earshot had certainly figured out long since that his professorial salary wasn't the whole story.

"It's not really the money," he'd explained as if he had to. "I want to find someone to share this plane with."

"Why bother?" sighed one of the reps, too far into his third double for discretion.

I watched Albert struggle with the problem of describing his Puritan ethic to a relative stranger, and a boozy one at that. He was, I felt mortally sure, consumed with guilt at the prospect of owning so conspicuous a symbol of the good life, but a little embarrassed to admit it. The Material Nineties were not the times to expose a social conscience. He settled for a half truth. "I don't have time to fly a lot. With someone else, maybe it won't sit around too much."

And that's how Parker LeMay had come into our lives. Someone from the party had told someone and within a day Parker had called Albert at his office. He would be very interested, he said, in sharing a plane if they could find one they both liked. Parker had flown in Vietnam. He couldn't look at a plane for a long time after that, he'd confessed, but now he was ready. He owned a small drug company of his own and that's how he'd heard about the conversation at the party. If Albert was serious, why not meet some morning at the general aviation airport and make some inquiries?

Why not indeed? Albert was thrilled, and not a little impressed at the prospect of sharing a plane with someone good enough to have flown in a war.

In due course, they found *Sweet Juliet*, rented hangar space, and arranged all the necessary systems of bookkeeping and scheduling. Now and then, when a decision had to be made about upkeep or buying fancy new gadgets, they spoke. Otherwise, their paths rarely crossed. We'd met Jann LeMay exactly twice. And now it looked like she and *Sweet Juliet* may have ended together.

The lunchroom, the destination we'd chosen to consider recent events, was more or less hiding in a back hall. I fished out some quarters and fed the machine. It produced two cups of very hot water lightly flavored with coffee, which we set on the single table. The lounge coffee would have been better but more public. We needed solitude. The small, barely furnished room was windowless but cheerful, a soft yellow paint brightening walls hung with torn T-shirt backs. An odd decoration, but one traditional in private airports. Flight instructors had used the shirts to commemorate first solos, those incredible moments when their students, without warning, found themselves alone in the plane and were told to take off on their own. *Mike M. broke free of ground by himself for first time, 9/12/92,* said one. *Barbara G. defeated gravity by herself on 4/14/96. David W. entered the pattern for the first time alone 6/16/86.* Upbeat, encouraging messages that did nothing for our spirits.

Albert had his head in his hands, which worried me. I wasn't used to seeing him show any signs of uncertainty. That, by mutual consent, was my job. He unfolded himself long enough to taste the coffee and made a face. A large carton of powdered cream was on the counter and he reached for it, pouring an obscene amount into the cup. "I sure wish the tower had a tape of that call."

"I thought only the Lear heard her. The tower didn't read it."

"That's the problem. So just hope as hard as you know how that this is a horrible mistake and the plane isn't ours." He stirred in the saturated fat. "Because if it is ours and Jann is in it, this crash is my fault."

"Yeah, right." I sighed. "And global warming is your fault. Maybe even nuclear winter." I shook my head in wonder. "It must be so exciting, being in charge of the universe and all."

He was still thinking out loud and ignoring me. "The plane came back last week from having its annual. I should have flown it first and I was going to, but Paul was having his science fair…. And, you know, I had to get those staff reports in." He stared miserably at the wall where a window should have been.

As little as I've allowed myself to know about flying, this time I knew what he meant. Once a year, by law, the plane had to be thoroughly inspected, which meant that once a year someone had to be the first to fly it after its hospital stay. And things sometimes go wrong when a plane is fooled with mechanically. One time, the gear wouldn't drop. The cabin signal said it had. Fortunately, as Albert started to land, the tower clued him in that the wheels were only partway down. Turned out to be a circuit breaker that had been accidentally tripped. Wonderful.

Now that the light was dawning, I looked at my husband with astonishment. "Are you telling me that we were going up today, together, for the first flight since the annual?" I stood up, unable to stay put in the face of this. "Oh, that's terrific. Let's not worry about something so incidental as orphaning our children. We could have been in that plane instead of your friend's wife."

"We'd have been fine. Besides, I have a lot more experience than Jann LeMay. I think."

I looked at this man, the love of my life and father of my children, and wondered again at all his contradictions. The part of him that was a basic scientist was cautious, careful, methodical. That was his mother's side, his Wasp side. Her family had founded the New England textile firm that provided a standard of living decidedly higher than many professors could enjoy. Generations of conservative thinkers had preserved the business, which was solid, if not exciting. It was providing a life for yet more generations through his sisters, their husbands, and children. The flair, however, came from his father, an atheistic Jew, gambler, inventor, wild man. I couldn't get enough of him on our annual winter trips back east. His passion for life ebbed not at all with time. He'd rave, stamping around the house, about Republican zealots and the folly of religion in all its forms. Albert had been sent for a year to a Unitarian Sunday school, strictly to learn Bible stories and only because the Bible was the underpinning of so much of Western culture.

Surprisingly, his mother, not his father, had bought him the fine Cremona-made violin with which he still played Tuesday night string quartets. The purchase was one of the few flamboyant gestures he could ever remember her making and he had been deeply touched by it. As was true of many who had been born wealthy, his mother saw very little to be gained by spending money. The shoemaker in their small town was used to repairing her handbags until there was nothing left to stitch. Her figure never changed and consequently neither did her wardrobe. Three Jamaican housemaids who worked for different families in the area were known to place bets before an event, guessing which of Mrs. Beckmann's four good suits would show up on a particular day. She was, in her understated way, quite a love.

But I didn't want her or any of our parents raising our children. I was just catching my breath for another explosion of outrage when a rap on the open door stopped me. Tom Fetherhof peered in uncertainly. "Am I interrupting something?"

It was an interruption for which Albert was visibly grateful. He'd met Tom as part of a double-blind drug study and, being already in his flying phase, had been delighted to find he was an FAA air safety inspector. Tom, it turned out, had been part of the investigative team for several highly publicized accidents. Albert jumped up and grabbed his hand, all gloom and the vestiges of our argument dispelled.

"Good to see you. You're here because of the crash, right?"

"Well, yes and no." Tom's words came deliberately with softened edges. A sandy-haired former Texan, he had an accent too laid-back for his job. "Can't say I didn't hear somethin' about it, though. Thought I'd drop by since I was in the neighborhood."

I'd met Tom somewhere casually, maybe at one of the few movies we managed to see. It wouldn't have been at a chamber music concert or any of the other high-culture hangouts Albert frequented with me reluctantly in tow. Tom was not the type. Wherever it was, however, Albert had introduced him to me with great pride of possession. *Look,* he seemed to say, *what great people I get to meet at work.*

"How are you, Tom?" I asked. "Want a cup of this flavored water? I think we have a few more quarters floating around."

"Thanks, no," he said. "I'm just on my way over to Flight Service. Thought I'd pop in. This isn't my gig, but..." He didn't really have to explain. You always know it when people love their jobs. "So what are you guys doing here? Why ain't you up in the air, Doc? Nice day like this."

"Funny you should ask. We're waiting to hear something about the crash, too. Our plane's gone missing on us and, well, we sorta wonder if that's our ELT going off."

"Missing?" His face, leathered by years in the sun, wrinkled into surprise. "Gee, that's too bad. Wow." He ran his hand through the light, thin hair.

"But unless you're planning to set up some cots in here, you'd be just as well off waiting at home. These things take time."

I had the sudden image of a whole extra day and, potential tragedy or not, I could use it. "How much time?" I asked hopefully. "It's already been, probably, two hours since *Sweet Juliet* was taken."

"Three days to get solid information sometimes. They're real careful about releasing it. Goes through channels. What do you mean 'taken'?"

We told him. He just shook his head. "Well, better her than you."

"Actually, we were just discussing that." I smiled sweetly up at Albert.

"So anyway," Tom hurried on, sensitive to the moment, "figure about four hours to find the plane. The sheriff in the area or a search party, they do the looking. That's why they tell people to stay with the plane. Four hours isn't all that long. The lady, if it really is a lady and not some guy with a high voice, she might be okay. But if she's dead, they'll call the FAA for permission to remove the body. And they'll get the permission so long as they leave the area cordoned off. Then they have to inform the family. So you see, you'd be here a good long time. And I wouldn't want to contact the husband just now if I were you, not till he has a chance to find out what's going on. Afraid no one's going to care much about you even if it is your plane."

"My, that's comforting."

"Tell you what," said Tom. "If you hear something more and can't get any information confirmed,

call me here.'' He handed Albert his card. ''That's
my mobile number. Maybe I can be of some help.
Hey, I owe ya. Those pills they gave me after the
study, you know? I've been using them ever since.
They're pretty good.''

"Great. Glad the stomach's better." You'd think
now and then my husband the doctor might forget
which pain belonged to which patient, but not Albert. I can run off my Visa, including the expiration
date, and just about all numbers, but that's my only
claim to mnemonic fame. Albert remembers what
we ate the morning of our honeymoon and how, in
detail, we spent the night before. It's a trial.

The two men shook hands again and agreed to
touch base if necessary. Tom, released from social
obligations, hurried off. We headed home, taking
our contradictory feelings with us.

As it happened, we didn't need to wait three days
for news.

The call, when it came, shocked us both and not
only because of its message. Real life had roared
back at us by late afternoon. Since we were so pow-
erless to do anything about the morning events, we'd
both made a real effort to push them out of our
thoughts. We were so deeply into our domestic
problems, such as they were, that the missing plane
had almost migrated to the back burner.

Millie, our housekeeper, was less than thrilled to
see us return. She hadn't planned dinner since we
were, after all, supposed to be off staring at Devil's
Tower. She'd had her evening of leisure all worked
out. A bratwurst sandwich eaten on her lap and wall-

to-wall sitcoms on the tube. She loved them all, the
Seinfelds and Frasiers and Murphy Browns and Cy-
bills. I'm sure she found them vastly more charming
than me, but then she hadn't known them as long.

Millie had helped my mother raise me. She'd
been part of the family for so many years, any il-
lusion I might have had of being in control of my
own household had been squelched the day she appeared at our door. A tall, big-boned woman whose
age I never knew, she'd have followed my mother
right into the senior citizen complex if they'd have
let her. That not being possible, she did the next best
thing and moved in with us. There was never a question of saying no. My kids ignore approximately
seventy percent of everything I say. They listen to
Millie, if only because they realize she has a direct
pipeline to their grandmother.

I talked to my mother every morning promptly at
seven-fifteen. That was nine-fifteen where she was
in Baltimore, and breakfast at the Oakhurst Retire-
ment Village was over. Half the time, when we were
through with our daily update, she asked to speak
with Millie. Then, after Millie took the portable
phone into another room, I'd hear whispered conversation, doubtless a report on every foolish thing
I'd done since yesterday. In the real world I was a
woman of reasonable confidence and some professional success. To them, I was still eight. They were
a pair, those two. They'd made it through more than
a few hard times together, most particularly the
wholly unexpected death of my father. Besides, they

belonged to the same generation. They shared references. I didn't really resent their relationship. Not too much.

Hah.

To her credit, Millie didn't make her displeasure at our return too obvious. We told her about the events of the morning, assuring her that we would graze our way through lunch and take the boys out for a Mexican dinner. "Seinfeld" reruns and the bratwurst thus secured, she seemed philosophically resigned. As for the missing plane, she'd been at me since I was four about not taking care of my toys. I could construct tomorrow's portable phone conversation. I made a mental note to be sure to tell my mother about *Sweet Juliet* so she wouldn't hear it from Millie first.

With our weekend now canceled and a pickup lunch dispatched, Albert began spending the rest of the day looking for ways to avoid the Siberian expanse of his study. He had started his sabbatical a week before and was trying to adjust to working at home. We had a year before life would restore itself to normal. The plan was for him to spend the first six months on library research and the last six on the road to an epidemiologist's dozen of third-world countries, each dirtier and more impoverished than the last. For better or worse, we were expected to go along. He'd already spoken to the head of the twins' private school, who concurred that the experience would be a marvelous education for sixteen-year-olds. I'd run the itinerary past several of my regular editors and had a number of possible article ideas ready to research. I'd also become an authority on exotic diseases and how to spot them. Not cure them. They weren't curable. Just spot them. I wanted to know what we'd be dying of.

The sabbatical which had sounded so utopian in theory was already turning into a problem of self-control. In the study was a desk and books and a good leather chair. Out here was life. The boys were normally home from school by three-thirty, full of noise and high drama. We both had enough discipline to stay at our writing till lunch, but then who could bear it? The fall days called us. I was terribly conscious that he was somewhere in the house and I could be with him. He had the same problem. With both of us home, concentration was turning out to be impossible. This sabbatical was going to be the ruin of us.

Having been given a "found" day, as well as a reprieve from flying, I'd decided to do something productive and was fooling around the late garden. We were on the back deck surrounded by trees in their October glory, and the events of the morning were temporarily tucked away. Several acres girded our sanctuary, successfully buffering the few neighboring houses. We kept more of the garden than necessary in flower and vegetable beds, making our summers sinfully water-intensive. Fall demanded massive cleanups. Now and then we felt guilty.

The cushions had been removed from the furniture and stored for the winter, but the year-round webbed chairs were fine and firm for Albert. I was painting out the chips on enamel pots, working on the picnic table. Albert stretched lazily, then settled into a slanted chair. "Is this the afternoon for the boys' tennis practice?" he asked, knowing perfectly well that tennis day was Wednesday.

"This is the afternoon for lectures on taking the PSATs," I said, not looking up from the delicate job. "They'd prefer tennis."

And as if on cue, the boys chose that moment for their entrance, emerging from the house with turkey and cheese sandwiches dripping dill pickle juice. Millie's treat. I hadn't seen any leftover turkey when I'd scrounged for our lunch. She must have hidden it. We might starve, but with Millie in charge, Paul and Spence will always fatten up nicely.

They had their father's slightly disjointed moves as well as strong hints that someday they could safely aspire to his good looks. While technically not identical, they caused outsiders great difficulty in telling them apart. Both were tall and skinny with fair skin and dark hair like Albert's. Their father, of course, had filled out (a nice euphemism) since his teen years, but early pictures showed him to be almost scrawny. He dressed with great care, however, putting me to shame. The twins, on the other hand, both favored black in all things sartorial. They usually looked like hired mourners at a funeral.

"Aren't you home awfully early?" asked Albert, trying to consult a watch he'd left on the bedside table.

"A little," said Spence, swiping at a drop of mustard on his chin. "They read us the riot act about the importance of the College Boards and then let us go,'' said Paul, finishing the thought. ''And these are just the PSATs. Wonder what'll happen next year when the things will actually count for something.''

''They'll shake. They'll wet their pants,'' added Spence with satisfaction.

''Spence, please.'' Albert, no prude about bodily functions, hated them verbalized casually.

''Well, Dad, you know they will. Private schools have to get the numbers and the PSATs do count.'' He picked up a small stone that had found its way onto the patio and hurled it toward the driveway with a practiced arm. ''National Merits are given for them and lists are published in the papers. We screw up, they go broke, sorta. Anyway, Pauly will uphold the honor of the school and everyone will remain happily employed. Hey, what are you guys doing home anyway?''

We explained the situation very briefly, not dwelling on the possibility that their parents might have been the ones flying a defective plane. We suspected that, minus the dramatic elements, the story wouldn't hold their attention long. But then sixteen-year-olds are full of surprises.

''We met Jann LeMay once, Mom. I told you,'' said Paul, surprisingly serious. ''She came to speak at a Career Day. She works for the governor.''

''A very foxy lady.'' Spence worked his eyebrows Groucho style. ''And she was wearing this Chinese-like dress, skintight. High neck. Way cool.''

"Well, like maybe she's Chinese, dorkhead."

"She isn't. She's Vietnamese. She told us that day."

Albert was belatedly tuning into the conversation. "What was she doing at Career Day? And that's interesting that she told you about being Vietnamese. I've always had the feeling she didn't want to talk about those days." He turned to me. "I asked her once if she'd been caught in the worst of it. She found a graceful way of ignoring me."

"She was there to represent public relations and press liaisons, that sort of thing," said Paul. "She's the governor's press secretary, gets to travel with him and everything. The fact that the gov was up for reelection that year may have had something to do with the reason she showed up. Mr. Beardsley was happy about that, about her coming, that is." Colin Beardsley was Dean of Students and the man who seemed to have drawn our number for fund-raising purposes. "It was real funny, though. I went up to her afterward and tried to ask a question and she, like, jumped back. I wonder if maybe she doesn't like kids."

Spence took a full watering can from the bench where I was working and poured a generous splash over his pickle-scented hands. He dried them on his black jeans and stretched hard. "Whatever, that is one gorgeous babe. Bet her husband's careful not to leave her alone too long."

"Hey, if she's really the one in the crashed plane, looks like he won't have to worry about it anymore,'' chortled Paul. Tasteless humor was their specialty.

Obviously, we didn't have to concern ourselves that they might overreact to our news. They loped off in the direction of the unsold acre that served the neighborhood kids as a sandlot, leaving us to digest their take on the situation. My brief meetings with Jann LeMay were long enough for me to register her good looks, but I needed my kids' hopping hormones to tell me about her effect on the opposite sex. So she was pretty. She also had to be pushing forty, since Parker had met her during the war. Granted, she didn't look it. That great Asian skin. Oh well.

I glanced over at Albert who seemed to be in an alpha state, and went back to my painting. I had three pots finished and was just starting on the fourth when the phone rang. Albert had finally dozed off in the warm sun. He jumped. When he'd been a young house officer on call, the sound of the phone had done just that to him. Then, he'd been afraid of what emergency the call might bring. Today, apparently, he was again. He clicked on the portable.

''Hello? Parker, is that you? What? Oh, no.'' His face collapsed. ''Wait, I can't hear you on this phone.'' He started for the house, throwing me a look that pretty much told the story. I put down the painting supplies and started in slow motion to clean up. Obviously, the pastoral part of the afternoon had just ended. Maybe we should have ignored Tom Fetherhof's advice and called Parker anyway. Maybe he'd just discovered that his wife was missing. Maybe he just learned that she'd taken the plane. Maybe that was all the call was about.

But I knew it was more.

Albert came back outside and sat down slowly on the edge of a redwood bench. "They found our plane. Crashed. His wife was in it."

"Is she...?"

"No. She's dead." Both eyes squeezed shut, he buried his head in his hands.

I went cold. It didn't matter that we hardly knew this woman. Her husband was associated in a way with Albert and, of course, it was our plane. It was our crash, our death. Finally I asked, "Do they know what happened?"

"If they do, they're not saying. Parker only knows that the woman in the plane was carrying Jann's identification. He assumes it's her. They're not telling him anything else yet."

"But it was definitely *Sweet Juliet?*"

"Apparently that much is certain. He's going to go up there and claim the body. Can you imagine?" He looked up, squinting in the sun. "He said he was told it would be several days before the details were known. He also said he didn't give a darn anyway. She was dead and that was all that mattered. He was crying. It was bad."

I went over to sit beside him and took his large square hand in mine. "I'm so sorry, love. Sorry for him and sorry for you that you had to get that call." I stared out past the trees to a far horizon. "But we've always known flying a small plane is a risk. It was a risk she accepted, that's all."

"No." Albert's face darkened, a cloud across the landscape. "Something is wrong here. This *wasn't* normal risk. Don't forget she basically stole the plane. Don't forget she broke all the rules of takeoff. None of this is making sense."

He was right, of course, but it hardly mattered. It didn't change the bottom line.

THREE

SWEET JULIET was history. We could see parts of her before we even reached the site of the wreckage, little pieces like a bolt, a side panel, the tip end of the propeller. They lay scattered through the mountain growth like exotic bits of foliage. Even so, we weren't prepared for the final devastation.

We'd waited through a tense Saturday, wanting to do something, feeling we should be at the scene, and knowing just how unwelcome our presence would be. The authorities said flatly, stay away. Parker didn't return Albert's calls. We spent the day starting projects and abandoning them. Concentration was gone, kaput.

Albert had left a message for Tom Fetherhof right after Parker hung up Friday, and in due time Tom returned it. He promised to let us know as soon as it would be possible to drive out to see the plane. By the time he called Sunday morning, we were so jumpy our kids had wisely decided to stay as far away as possible. They bailed out around ten, an hour that rarely found them even fully awake, and headed in the general direction of friends' saner houses. After talking to Tom, we left them a note saying that we were going to the crash site and not to bother Millie about lunch. She was home, of course, but technically Sunday was her day off. Reluctantly, we knocked on her door in the east wing of the house and told her we were leaving. She grunted through the paneled wood and we backed away quickly. Now and then I dream about a servile housekeeper from the old school....

The plane, Tom said, had gone down about eighty miles west of the city in an area known for the mountains' abrupt rise from the valley floor. We filled the Aurora with its favorite high-test and headed out, not certain why we had to see the mess, but very sure that we couldn't do anything else until we did. We were able to approach within a mile or so by passable road, but the rest of the way was a hike in. When we stepped out of the car, the chilly air attacked. Though fall had come only lightly to the plains, it was well established here in the higher elevations. Fresh snow, maybe two inches, glistened in the noon sunlight, scrunching under our hiking boots like crushed ice. The vegetation was thick, mostly pines and the bare trunks of aspen groves crossing at odd angles, making footsteps difficult. The sound of voices came to us even before we spotted the broken airplane parts, and we turned left toward the noise.

Two men were standing near the crash site, talking. They looked up when they sensed our approach and started over. Unflustered but wary, I decided. We told them who we were and why we'd come but the wariness remained.

"I'm Tim Harding and this here's Rocky Delmonico. We're from the sheriffs department in Alameda," said the older of the two, a paunchy western type with low-slung, sagging chinos. I glanced at Albert's leather bomber jacket, open to reveal a buff yellow knit shirt. For once it was okay that he looked prettier than I did. I was in grunge jeans and a knockabout windbreaker, looking suitable. I decided to do the talking. Now and then I can be a pushy broad.

"Any idea what happened here?" I looked at the men like someone who deserved answers. "I know you guys aren't in charge of the investigation, but maybe, you know... Heard anything?" I was losing confidence under their stare.

Rocky, the younger of the two, came through as thin, dark, and dangerous. "Yeah, maybe." His eyes swept me head to toe before turning to Albert. Then he answered my question, looking straight at him. Real men don't talk business to women. Not this real man. I was willing to bet no one had ever accused these guys of being politically correct.

"We might have heard the plane types talkin' about some kind of trouble here," he said, smug as a kid with a dirty picture. "Like maybe the accident was, could be, deliberate. 'Course, can't say that for sure since we're not mechanics." He stepped sideways and glanced around.

Albert seemed about to react to that extraordinary piece of information when his eyes followed the other man's look and he lost the words. That was when we got our first view of the plane we'd flown so many times, our bumpy magic carpet to offbeat destinations and odd adventures. The sight took our breath away. Inexplicably, I felt tears well up.

Slowly, shocked, we walked toward the tangled mess of metal. The little Piper had obviously been moved since it struck the ground. We could see where it had hit from the depression in the dirt, a surprisingly wide swath of torn-up sand and ground cover ending in a hole three feet deep where the nose had burrowed in. It lay now on its side, the fuselage broken, its edge thrust into the cabin with horrifying authority. The once shiny beige paint was crackled, a natty orange-and-brown stripe that once ran the length of the plane now twice separated. The left wing was completely torn off. We couldn't see where it had landed. It was simply gone. The right wing was almost untouched. From a certain angle, it looked like a giant hand could come and pick the plane up like a toy, righting it to fly again. We moved closer and cautiously peered inside.

The blood was obvious and startling. I found myself making a funny noise and grabbing Albert's arm. Then I looked again quickly, a kid peeking at a scary movie through almost closed fingers. At second glance, the quantity of blood seemed diminished. The worst splashes were against the top of the cabin, but both seats had received their share. Something undefined, possibly specked with bone, had landed on the floor under the passenger seat where it had been apparently overlooked by whoever had removed the body and straightened up the scene. I found a rock nearby and sat down, dropping my head between my knees.

"When I first saw it, her body was still in it." The voice caused our heads to snap around as if we'd been caught shoplifting. It was a familiar voice but strained. A controlled Parker LeMay was walking up the path, followed closely by the mechanic Jack Potts. "I'll never forget it. Not for the rest of my life."

I managed to stand and we walked over together to greet the new widower whose wife had suffered such a terrible end. "Parker," said Albert, taking the man's hand, "we're so dreadfully sorry." His approach was warm and concerned. If he still felt guilt, he wisely concealed it. I muttered something, the usual something.

LeMay didn't look up. He seemed to be checking his heavy boots for rocks, banging one against a fallen log to dislodge the muck. "Thank you," he said, meeting no one's eye. "And please be assured that the annual had nothing to do with it. I understand you were concerned on that score." How had he heard that? The world of recreational pilots must have some kind of grapevine. "Besides," he continued, "the NTSB seems to think, if you can believe this, that someone tampered with the plane, with the elevator cable." He raised his head and we saw the face of absolute grief. His eyes seemed sunken in their sockets, circled by lines not so much red as a shadowy black. For the second time in fifteen minutes, I felt tears rise.

LeMay was in his late forties, still slim, with a full head of slicked-back hair. The color was hard to determine, the mousy-gray tint that once was blond. His small mustache had gone predominantly white. He was wearing a dark winter parka zipped to the neck though the temperature was now at least in the fifties. It seemed as though he thought he'd never get warm. He might have appeared passingly handsome if he'd been able to rid himself of the nervous habits that so marked his manner. He laughed inappropriately, a deadly mistimed giggle that stopped conversation. His movements were jerky and uneven, giving him an edgy quality. No one could believe he'd flown in 'Nam. He didn't seem to have the temperament.

Still, he'd obviously returned with a war bride, the beautiful Jann, or whatever her name was in the old country. All of us who knew him recognized how totally he worshiped her. She was his whole life, his purpose, his only joy. No children. This was the kind of marriage that had no room in it for any-one else. Exclusive. Self-absorbed.

And now he'd lost her.

Jack Potts had stayed a few steps behind waiting for the appropriate condolences to end. Now he moved into the circle. "Hi, Doc," he said quietly. "Mrs. B."

The men from the sheriff's office chose this mo-ment to make their important presence known. They both lit cigarettes as if on cue and approached the four of us. "Harding and Delmonico. We met yes-terday at the sheriff's office," they said to LeMay. "Is there something more we can help you with?"

LeMay came back from his reverie. "Yeah. We want to look around. I want Jack here to take a look at the engine. I want to check the cabin. I've heard it's okay to do this now." He hesitated a moment and then rushed the next words. "If there was anything in the plane, what happened to it? I mean, do you guys have whatever she left behind?"

Rocky Delmonico looked very happy to have a mission. I was happy he had a mission, too, as long as it took him far, far away. Funny how fast a joker like that can turn me off. He stepped forward, bristling with importance. "Let me go back to the office and see what happened to the stuff that was in the plane. I know there were some things, okay? The Feds may have left the stuff with us. They looked at everything already."

"Like what?" asked LeMay.

"Like a purse. Some kind of package. Funny, you know? This plane is all smashed up, and the woman is all smashed up, and the lipstick doesn't even have its top off." The sheriff's man realized too late how that sounded. This guy hadn't read the chapter on tact. He backed away, trying to distance himself from his own stupid comment. "I'll drive into town and get whatever you can have. Bring it to you. It'll take me about a half hour."

Albert was still talking to LeMay and Potts so I drifted off toward Tim Harding. The smell of his cigarette, even when cut by too much fresh air, was drawing me to him. I had the wild thought of asking him for a puff, but rejected it. Seven years and it still smelled great. I was fine with not smoking, providing no one else did. I watched with seriously mixed feelings as he threw down the half-finished butt and ground it against a rock. Too late. Oh well, I needed to talk to him anyway. Alone.

"So were you here when the Feds first came?" I asked casually.

His wariness flashed, flared, and disintegrated. I looked too sweetly innocent to be dangerous. "We brought 'em up here. We're the ones who found the wreck, after all. They wouldn't have been worth a whole heck of a lot without us," he added, straightening slightly.

I couldn't let this opportunity pass without milking it for any information I could turn up. What was this about something in the plane being tampered with? Maybe they weren't supposed to tell Parker or us that, but since they had, there was no way any of us could forget it. Could the crash really have been deliberate, a successful attempt at sabotage? An even bigger question slipped ominously to the surface. We were supposed to be the ones flying. Did someone want us dead? Jann wasn't supposed to take the plane, we were. Her odd behavior, her strange theft of the Piper, had apparently saved our lives.

I needed to know all this quiet sheriff's man would tell me. "How did she look when you found her?" I asked him, trying not to sound too morbid. "I mean, well…unusual at all?"

"She looked dead. That's how she looked. There was sure no question about her having survived the crash."

"So just that. Nothing else?"

"Well…" He scratched a bite that was rising angrily on his wrist. "I suppose there was something, though I'm sure it didn't mean nothing. I mentioned it to Rocky. He'd noticed it, too. The lady had funny patches of skin on the leg I was able to see. Kind of wrinkled and discolored, but not like sunburn or anything. Of course, we didn't move the body. The Feds took care of it.''

I stared at the nearby mountains, trying to make sense of this bizarre fact. Interesting, too, that both men had noticed. It must have been fairly distinctive. "Could she have been burned? Did the plane catch fire at all?''

"It didn't. Not at all. We thought of that, too, but there wasn't no fire. Gotta hand it to the lady. She had control of the plane to the end. She must have put it down soft enough, at least, not to explode. If there'd been a fire, we'd have been lucky to find out who'd been killed. I mean, it would have taken a while. Dental records, stuff like that. No, the stuff on her leg looked like some kind of awful skin disease. My wife's aunt had psoriasis but this was worse. But like I said, I doubt it means anything.''

"Interesting.'' Skin diseases seemed a little irrelevant. I tried a different tack. "What about luggage? Was there anything in the plane?''

"You mean like a suitcase? Naw, nothing. They took some kind of package out of the back, that little cargo area, but that's all. Except for her purse, like Rocky said.''

That package again. Probably the one Jack Potts had seen. It wouldn't explain the crash, but it might have something to do with Jann's escapade. Before I could ask about it, Albert, LeMay, and Jack Potts started toward the plane and us. Albert moved to my side, but I wasn't looking at him. I was watching Parker LeMay. Potts was starting to check the engine, a bag of tools beside him, his clean, delicate fingers beginning to probe the bent metal. The cowling had been torn off on one side, making access easier. But it was LeMay's actions I found curious. He had moved to the cargo space behind the rear seat and had both hands in there groping. Since the plane was lying on its left side, the door to that area was accessible. Normally it would be locked. I hadn't noticed if the crash had sprung it open. Of course, Parker would have a key. He owned half the plane. Still, he must have been thinking clearly to bring it with him. That is, assuming he unlocked the door himself. I cursed myself for not noticing these details, since I was beginning to feel that what had happened here might be absolutely critical to our lives. Once I realized how close to death we had come, everything to do with this accident had become very compelling.

I was, after all, a journalist of sorts, used to detail. Time, in fact past time, to start using my skills.

FOUR

LeMay CAME UP empty-handed from his search. He sat back on his heels, then turned and saw me watching. "I thought maybe they left something behind," he said, going back to his knees. Like a blind man, he poked around some more under the seat and then gave it up. I hoped he hadn't seen all the blood and gore, but there was no way he could have missed it. With the broken fuselage, the interior of the main cabin had been pretty thoroughly destroyed. He stood, stepped back, and brushed himself off. The day was warming rapidly, but apparently he barely felt it. He opened the top of the heavy winter parka but didn't remove it. I was dying to talk to Albert alone but he moved away. Now he was hunkering with Jack Potts over the remains of his beautiful engine.

I took my eyes from LeMay, to what I thought was his obvious relief, and wandered toward the front of *Sweet Juliet*. Potts and Albert had their heads together. I found a patch of grass nearby and moved close enough to hear. My liberal arts education didn't include any courses in engines, not the kind that power planes, not even the kind that power cars. I didn't even know enough to fake it, but I listened hard.

"It's been cut," Potts was saying. "You can see

it clearly right here. The edge is too smooth.'' He was pulling on the end of a dark cable, stroking the outside with a finger.

To me, the engine looked big enough for a go-cart. Certainly no self-respecting car operated with such a minimal power source. Grimly, on one knee, Albert stared into the innards behind the propeller. "Would that have caused the crash?"

"Maybe. But the elevator cable didn't have to do the job alone. Look in here. There's been more tampering. Still, without the elevator working, she wouldn't have been able to get the plane up when she needed to." Potts sat back, wiping his hands on his pants. "My guess is that whoever cut it, deliberately didn't cut it through. It was okay when she started out. But then, once she needed the altitude to get over the fourteeners, the strain finished the job. The cable split. Didn't she say on the radio that the plane wouldn't respond?"

"Something like that."

"Whoever did it had the timing pretty well figured out. What they hadn't figured was..." He glanced up at me and stopped talking.

"Go ahead and say it, Jack," I said angrily. "We know what you're thinking. They hadn't figured that we wouldn't be taking the plane."

He looked away and didn't answer.

Albert stood, brushing at his pant legs with great care. "So, Gracie." He grinned. "Who've you been infuriating lately? The cleaner? The lawn man? Somebody you wrote about in an article?" The possibility of the latter slowed him for a moment.

"Didn't you do a piece on tax evaders? Anger any right-wing zealots lately? Or left-wing?"

He was only half kidding. The Rocky Mountain states were developing a reputation of sorts. The hills were alive with the sound of psychotics.

"Why me? Maybe some of your patients hate long waits."

"My patients recognize perfection. They'll wait." Albert reached over, hands extended, I gave him mine, and he pulled me up off the uneven ground. Then he took me in his arms and held me tight, half reassurance and half something else. I relished the moment. Still, it was an undercurrent of fear that was resonating between us and no amount of banter could hide it.

Suddenly, Rocky Delmonico came crashing through the underbrush carrying two plastic supermarket bags, one on each side. "Got the stuff for you, Mr. LeMay. They said you could have it since the big government men had already cleared it. We think that you should keep it somewhere and not throw it out," he added with a touch of self-importance. "Just in case they may need it again."

Curious, we watched Parker empty the bags. If he was uncomfortable doing so in front of so many people, he seemed to consider it the better part of valor to pretend otherwise. The first bag contained a woman's purse, a Louis Vuitton. The inside was hard to see for everyone but Parker, who was going through it quickly. He pulled out a wallet, still fastened, opening the money compartment without much interest. The credit cards he spent more time with, separating them and looking at each. His touch on the plastic was almost a caress, as if evoking the hand of the woman who owned each one. A small memo, folded in fourths, was tucked between an ATM card and one for United Airlines' Mileage Plus. Parker unfolded the page, glanced at the penciled message, and pocketed it. It's not easy being nosy when you're only five four. I was trying so hard to read over his shoulder, I almost lost my balance and fell on him. Jack Potts righted me with a gentle smile of amusement.

What I'd seen was a telephone number, 42-something something, but I hadn't caught all the figures. I wanted that piece of paper. Don't ask me why. I just wanted it. LeMay wasn't entitled to any secrets about this crash when we were the ones targeted for extinction. He'd shoved it deep into the zippered pocket of his parka from where, even though the zipper wasn't closed, it was unlikely to fall out. Darn.

Parker finished with the purse and reached for the other plastic bag. In it, along with loose brown paper, was what looked like a plastic cylinder that opened in the center. Its size was roughly that of a quart of transmission oil. The hollowed middle was empty when LeMay twisted the halves apart. An emotion of some sort seemed to catch him and he looked away.

"What is that, Mr. LeMay?" asked Tim Harding. "We was wondering when we first saw it."

"I'm...not sure. It could...I don't know."

Yeah, right. I didn't believe him for a moment. I

caught Albert's eye and gave him my "give me a break" look. He shrugged. Husbands can be obtuse at times.

LeMay put the two halves of the cylinder back together and returned it to the plastic bag, setting it near the other one with the Louis Vuitton. He turned to Potts and Albert. "So what did you guys find in the engine?"

The three of them went back to the wreck. Harding and Delmonico, once more lighting fresh cigarettes, muttered something about getting back for Sunday dinner with the family. Tim Harding, noticing the way I watched the matches flicker against the beautiful tobacco, pulled the pack from his pocket again and held it out to me. Did I suggest that this man wasn't sensitive? If we'd been alone together, I'd have accepted in a heartbeat. The situation was stressful enough to provide a more than ample excuse. Alas, I said no thank you. They called out good-byes and took off down the trail toward their official sheriff's car with its comforting bells and whistles.

The midday sun was working on my empty stomach. We'd been too nervous to eat breakfast. Groping in the pocket of my windbreaker, I turned up one of those wagon-wheel red-and-white mints tucked in a corner and popped it in my mouth. The jacket, completely synthetic, was great when the water was falling outside. Now it was a sauna. I took it off and tied the sleeves around my waist, checking to make sure another of those comforting mints didn't drop from a pocket.

It was very warm now, maybe in the high seventies, with the air motionless. Had Parker LeMay felt the heat enough to remove his heavy parka? I looked over at the cluster of men huddled around Jack Potts and the autopsied engine. LeMay was in shirtsleeves. Where was his jacket? I spotted the navy-and-black parka near the two plastic bags where he'd apparently tossed it.

I sauntered toward the bags, all casual nonchalance. I waited till the three men's heads were practically inside the cowling, then quickly groped for the paper, sliding my hand through the slit in the parka's left side. My fingers touched grit, which lodged under my nails, and then something metal and hard. Car keys. Wrong pocket. I stopped, checked the men at the plane again, and tried the other side. Bingo. I felt the paper from Jann's purse. Carefully, I removed it. Palming it for a second till I could be sure no one would look up, I unfolded the sheet with sweaty fingers.

The paper was from a standard three-by-five memo pad, the kind used in many offices. This one, however, had the state seal in one corner. The twins had said Jann worked for the governor. On it was a single phone number. I committed it to memory on the spot. Mine, as I said, was the kind of mind that could forget her mother's maiden name but had no problem reeling off the whole family's social security numbers. Figures stayed with me. Seven figures were nothing. I had them.

The paper was still in my hand, folded again,

when Parker LeMay looked up and noticed me near his stuff. He frowned. "Are you looking for something, Grace?"

Now all three men were staring at me. "No, no, nothing at all. It's just shady here under this tree." I smiled foolishly.

The men turned back to their work, Parker more slowly than the others. The memo felt like it was burning my palm. I couldn't get rid of it quickly enough. One swift movement and it was back in the right-hand pocket of the parka. Elated, my lungs inflated gratefully. Maybe proper women pushing forty weren't made for thievery, but then I wasn't that proper. For sure, one of the first things I was going to do when we got home was call that number. It was probably nothing, Jann's pager or the governor's. But Parker LeMay had been eager to find and remove it from his wife's wallet and that meant Grace Beckmann was going to find out whose it was. Period.

Suspicion grows like one of those trick sponges soaked in water, swelling till it takes over the bowl. Stolen planes, cut cables, fatal air crashes—why were these crazy things happening to us? When my kids were little and coming down with strange illnesses (not, of course, the obvious ones), I never simply relied on their pediatrician to diagnose them. I'd hit the medical library and *Cumulative Index Medicus* to dope it out for myself.

I felt the same way now. There was a threat out there, a real one. I sensed harm about to come to me or mine. I couldn't just trust someone else to care about the outcome. Self-reliance is the only child's greatest asset. And biggest curse.

I might have to remind Albert again, and soon, about this need of mine and where it came from. When my mother was widowed, I was the one she turned to. She was a person who had never made a move without acquiring at least half a dozen conflicting opinions from her friends. Then, after that, my father usually made the decision without even consulting her. She expected me to step in, young as I was, with the same definitive ways she so admired in my father. So, of course, I did. Children learn quickly what is expected of them. Now, in adulthood, I was left with the feeling that if mistakes were to be made, I'd better be the one to make them. I could live with mistakes of my own. I just couldn't stand letting someone else screw things up for me.

Jack Potts was the first to leave. He came over to say good-bye. His hands were, at last, filthy. He was working hard with a checked handkerchief, trying to remove the engine oil now ground around each of his nails. It seemed an omen. Something dirty had happened and it was rubbing off on all of us. "It'll be okay," he said with a sweetness that surprised me. "We'll get to the bottom of this." He turned and was off, down the rocky trail, shifting a metallic gray bag full of tools to his back.

We left next, stepping carefully back down the uneven path, not really talking till we were safely in the Aurora and almost to the main highway. The magnitude of what we'd seen loomed in my mind like the Devil's Tower we never reached, huge and steep. I didn't know how to begin. Finally I settled on a direct route. "LeMay isn't telling us even part of what he knows."

The speed with which Albert answered told me he was tracking the same thought. "Do you doubt that he's grieving, though? I've never seen a more miserable man. If he's faking, he belongs at the Old Vic."

"I agree. He's devastated. But he's still hiding something. That piece of plastic, for example. What was that?"

"Darned if I know."

"And the telephone number he purloined. But, of course, I've got that."

Albert negotiated the entrance ramp to the highway and settled into an even speed before turning to look at me. "Got it? What does that mean? Did you steal that piece of paper?"

"Indeed not. I memorized it. Parker acted like it was important so naturally I want to know why."

"Grace, listen, he handled that paper as subtly as possible, though I saw him fool with it, too. He didn't mention it and obviously I didn't ask. But he would have said plenty if he'd seen you going through his stuff. What did you think you were looking for? Some reason to hope that Jann was the intended victim of the crash instead of us?"

I fished a piece of Kleenex from the glove compartment and blew my nose, clearing it of mountain-induced congestion. Leaves were caught in my hair, which was due for its biannual cut. I pulled down the visor and peered into a mirror lit like a makeup table, picking twigs and debris from the thick, straight dark mass. Usually, I pulled it up into some kind of order, a braid or twist, but today I couldn't. Maybe tomorrow.

Albert went on thoughtfully. "It's far more likely that Potts is wrong about the slice on that cable. It was cut accidentally during the annual. Of course." He was quickly cheered. "Now that's a reasonable explanation. You know how things go wrong."

"Multiple things? Didn't Jack Potts say there was other tampering? And didn't those sheriff's guys say the Feds had implied, that too?"

Albert didn't answer but his smile faded. I opened the center armrest, with its collection of tapes, glasses, and instruction sheets, and removed the cellular phone, pulling up its antenna and flipping on the power.

"Calling to see how the kids are doing?"

"Calling my mystery number."

The car swerved slightly. Albert stared, and not at the road. "Please don't! What if someone answers? Gracie, what are you doing? LeMay is going to find out you've been interfering and come looking for us. Be a nice person and put that phone back." A car to the left honked, forcing Albert to concentrate on the highway. While he worked his way back to the correct lane, I dialed. The numbers were written clearly on my brain. I read them right off. Albert, realizing it was too late to stop me, strangled his objections under something that sounded like "Aarggggh."

Four rings, nothing, and then the click that announced an answering machine, the old kind, not the telephone company system. A fuzzy electronic sound and then, "Hi. This is Hallie. Please leave me a *really* nice message right after the beep." An image formed immediately, floating in space like a hologram. A succulent, slightly *zaftig* blond, the kind who spends her evenings reading *Cosmopolitan.* The beep was welcome, like salt on a margarita glass. Something to cut the syrup. I pushed the cell phone's power off and mimicked the message to Albert.

"All right!" he offered enthusiastically. "Sounds, as the boys would say, like a babe."

"You might say so. That phone number should have been in Parker's wallet, not Jann's."

We drove the rest of the way home in silence, both of us in deep thought. Albert, a believer in my instinctive powers, would have said I could hear his mind working. I've frightened him more than once by answering the questions he hadn't yet asked. When I was really on, I could tell what cards he kept during an occasional cribbage game. As for hearing his mind work right now, I certainly could. It sounded like a malfunctioning jackhammer.

The twins met us at the door into the house from the garage, smelling fairly ripe from an active morning. Teenage sweat can assault the nose. They had, as usual, some kind of food in one hand, a mid-afternoon snack, the one between the early-afternoon nosh and the late-afternoon nibble. "You've had a million calls," said Paul. "That wonderful Call Waiting kept interrupting me and Clarice. We hardly were able to finish the math homework." Paul, the overachiever, didn't need Clarice. For math, that is.

They handed us a list of messages, proud of their telephone efficiency. It took us years to get them to write things down, years during which I lost endless important information. Once they blew a whole assignment for me. I was grateful for the current improvement.

I scanned the list. The tennis game was moved to nine-thirty from nine in honor of cooler days. Call me when you can, Magda, the organizer, had added. By now, the girls had certainly heard and read all about the accident. Doubtless it had been the subject of talk amongst them, the general gist probably being if God had wanted man to fly little planes, he wouldn't have invented jumbo jets. Mother Beckmann had called wanting a recipe. We were going to have to catch her up on things. And a memorial service had been scheduled for tomorrow, Monday, for Jann LeMay. Someone from the family had called to tell us, the kids not noting who.

"Isn't that awfully early?" I asked Albert, who was excavating a cold bottle of Coke from the lowest refrigerator shelf.

"Four days. She was killed on Friday."

"Well then, good." I leaned back against the counter.

"Now what?"

"Now we meet some of the people in their lives. Maybe even the delicious Hallie."

"Oh, no." He shook his head and looked around for a bottle opener. "I sense trouble."

The kids had gone off again but even so I lowered my voice, not wanting anyone to overhear. I needed to invest the moment with all the seriousness it could bear. I touched Albert's shoulder, forcing him to look at me. "Don't you see, we have to get involved here. Something terrible is happening and we're part of it. Are you really willing to leave everything up to the authorities?"

"You mean authorities as in police? Yeah, I'm kinda willing to do that. But I'm sure you're not. It's not like you, more's the pity."

"It's not like you either."

He looked around for a clean glass, found none, and took a swig from the bottle, turning increasingly pensive as he did. "Well, okay, what the heck. I'll give it a week. See what we can find out. But that's it. I do have a few other things on the agenda, like a major sabbatical project."

I wasn't at all sure we could wrap things up in a week but one concession would do for now. I gave him a quick kiss and headed off for my bedroom closet. I needed to decide what one wears to a memorial service when the cause of death looks like murder.

FIVE

EVERYTHING ABOUT the memorial service seemed precipitous, like something to be whipped through. Funerals, for obvious reasons, couldn't wait forever. In Albert's family, they followed the Jewish tradition of putting the bodies in the ground quickly. That made evident sense. Memorial services, however, should require a bit of time, time to round up the speakers, time to think about honoring the dead. When my father was killed, there wasn't enough of the body left to bury, but it took us two weeks before we, my mother and I, could pull ourselves or a service together. Okay, I was only twelve and didn't have a lot of experience, but she always asked my advice and sometimes took it.

Well, but hey, this wasn't my party. If Parker wanted a quick closure, wanted to put this behind him, so be it. Monday at two o'clock found Albert and me at the city's largest mortuary chapel with about fifty other people, a couple obviously cops.

The crash story had run in the morning papers causing Albert, belatedly, to react to the ruin of his plane. The loss had been up till now overshadowed by a human death, but now he was in an added state of grief for *Sweet Juliet*. Like a kid whose bike has been stolen, he had trouble thinking of anything else. His next plane, and I was mortally sure there would be one, would not be shared. An experience like this was enough for one lifetime.

The first rays of morning sunshine, waking us together when it splayed across the pillows, found us changed by a halfway decent night's sleep. Our default mode had turned optimistic. We had spent the evening going over every aspect of our lives. Rationally, no one we knew could possibly want to kill us. Rationally, that is. Irrationality was still a wild card, as was the chance that we had an unknown enemy. Still, we felt that someone other than Albert or me was probably the intended victim. This was a biggie, this comforting and maybe delusional thought. Sometimes you can pose a problem to your mind just before you go to sleep and the mind will obediently come up with a solution by morning, but no one takes any bets that the solution actually works. The cut elevator cable, the tampered engine...even though they almost caught us, we were largely convinced they were meant for someone else. Jann? Maybe. Probably. But we absolutely had to know. After all, we could still be wrong. Pensively, we left for the chapel.

At my insistence, we found seats over to one side so I could have the best view of who was there. Light entered the hall weakly through stained-glass windows, coloring dust motes that hung in the air. The musty smell and piped-in music were dutifully depressing. I didn't know a soul. Jack Potts hadn't come, which surprised me slightly, but some men never go to death rites of any kind. Over half the audience was Asian, and they seemed to be sitting in a cluster, chatting together quietly before the service began. The rest seemed mostly to be men unaccompanied by wives, wearing sport coats over tieless shirts. Parker's work force, maybe, taking as brief a break from their projects as possible. A couple of bankers, judging from their vests and polished wingtips. Some youngish women, inexpensively chic, perhaps from the governor's office. All lapsed into silence when a clergyman of unknown denomination opened the proceedings with a generic prayer. Then the speakers were off, each in turn.

Some of Jann's coworkers participated, as well as a representative of the Vietnamese community apparently designated to speak for all immigrants from that once-beleaguered land. The middle-aged woman, small and deeply lined but with piercing dark eyes that held the small group transfixed, talked with pride about Jann's rise to her position of power. In the hardworking Vietnamese community, I thought, there must be many such stories of people transplanted to a culture they could hardly have imagined, but who managed to make it their own. Certainly Jann's own life, as her countrywoman told it, was a study in determination as well as ambition. Quite a tale, this, and one I hadn't heard. Parker, apparently, had not always been able to keep his elegant wife in designer silks.

After marrying LeMay and escaping 'Nam in '75, said the speaker, Jann, her name anglicized, settled with him here. She was then only eighteen and they were fairly desperate for money. She started working for an advertising agency as a night cleaning woman, a position that didn't require language. If she resented the life she had been forced to lead, no one ever heard her say so. Her husband was trying to start a business, incurring debts along the way, and those who knew her then had said she was proud that her paycheck was often what stood between them and real need. The years doing menial jobs provided more than just survival wages, however. Along the way, even while working largely at night, she learned not only English but also the advertising business. As soon as she could express the idea, she made it clear to her employers that she expected to move higher in the firm. Any surprise they may have felt at finding ambition in such an unlikely spot dissipated as they watched her work. Certainly, she had nowhere to go but up, and up she went. From janitorial work, she graduated to the mailroom, then receptionist, then assistant account executive. She knew, with her own instinctive taste as well as careful observation of the women she wanted to emulate, how to dress, how to look, how to stand. Not surprisingly, her specialty became public relations. Eventually, she was discovered and hired away by the then newly elected Governor Merriwell to be his press liaison, a job she'd held for the six years prior to her death.

"She was there for anyone from the Vietnamese community who needed help unsnarling the workings of the bureaucracy and she was a credit to her people." The tiny woman's black eyes flashed as she said this, daring anyone in the room to contradict her.

The colleagues who had spoken first had stressed Jann's reliability, her willingness to work whatever hours necessary, her dedication to the job. No one was the least bit weepy. In fact, the remarks were fairly superficial. No stories of life behind the scenes, of good times shared. I had the feeling no one, with the possible exception of the Vietnamese woman, really knew this lady, let alone cared about her. No one, that is, but Parker. He was sitting in the front row of the chapel with a few other people I didn't recognize. His head was bowed, and now and then his shoulders trembled slightly.

The altar was covered with flowers, large arrangements of salmon gladiolus, lilies, and alstroemeria, smaller ones of yellow asters and golden mums. From Parker's professional colleagues, I guessed. I poked Albert discreetly. "Obviously an ice goddess," I whispered. "Do you suppose she had any friends?"

He shrugged, lifting his thick brows.

I didn't catch the name of the clergyman who was running the show, a slender young man with an unfortunate Adam's apple. Whoever he was, he was apparently encouraged to invite everyone at the service over to the downtown loft where Parker lived. By now it was three in the afternoon. Albert tends to look at his watch obsessively when he's restless. Thus far he'd checked it five times. Before he could even suggest we go home, I informed him under my breath that of course we were going to Parker's place.

"We're on a mission, remember?"

"Heck." He slumped further into the plush seat. He didn't argue but his expression told me how little he thought of this waste of a day.

We filed out silently with the crowd, not looking back at the family, still in their seats. The Aurora was parked in lonely splendor on a side street where no one would ding it. We aimed its nose toward downtown.

The blocks of lofts, once warehouses and turn-of-the-century business buildings, had been converted to condos by the most forward-looking and creative of the city's developers. Jann, it seemed, had been savvy about trends. I'd heard it from the tennis girls when she and Parker had bought what became the penthouse unit in an old wholesale dairy. We wondered why anyone would want to live where there were no groceries, no cleaners, no support systems for ordinary life. Since then, the unit had probably quadrupled in value and contractors couldn't renovate the old buildings fast enough. Jann was no fool.

The penthouse, when we finally arrived, was stunning, windows on all sides overlooking the marvelous city skyline. Industrial chrome and steel set the tone, with four black-and-white sofas at angles in the large open spaces. The floor was unrelenting, varicolored stone polished to a high gloss. Here and there, small squares of pale rugs created islands of warmth. It was a fabulous place to visit. I wouldn't have wanted to live there.

About fifty or so people had come to the service, and about twenty were at the loft by the time we arrived. They were hovering in small groups around the glass dining room table which was covered with platters of smorgasbord, hors d'ouevre-style delicacies, and tiny cakes and filled puffs, precisely iced. A nice mid-afternoon repast for bored palates. I wondered who had catered. Parker was talking quietly in one corner, greeting a small stream of visitors. A maid with cascades of perfectly cornrowed hair was taking and delivering drink orders, most of which seemed to be of the seriously alcoholic variety even though the sun wasn't even kissing the yardarm. I heard someone call "LaShawn" and watched her head turn sharply. So she wasn't the caterer. I had a name. She must belong here, since someone knew her. For investigative purposes, household help might come in very handy indeed. I filed the name in my random access memory and availed myself of an artichoke bottom filled with a dab of crème fraîche and caviar.

By the time I wiped the last remnant of roe from my grateful lips, Albert was deep in conversation with our unmistakable First Politico. I hadn't seen him at the service but was pleased to see him here. Impressive that he had shown up himself and not simply sent a representative. Furthermore, he didn't seem to be making perfunctory handshakes and heading for the door. I wondered why, but whatever, Governor Robert "High-Country Bob" Merriwell was quite a commanding presence on or off camera. I moved to Albert's side and waited for an introduction.

Up close, the man was massive. Six four, at least,

and maybe two hundred seventy five pounds. A bald strip that ran along the part ended in a fine, bare expanse on the top of his head. It did nothing to detract, nothing at all. I wondered if Jann, working closely with him, had found him desirable. He'd been in office long enough for the gossip to be well established and it labeled him a total pragmatist, a man whose unexamined life bothered him not a whit. Politically, he'd been elected by Republicans who didn't really buy his family values package, but found him the lesser evil. What is it with these guys who push the electorate's conservative buttons? Don't they realize they're likely to be hoisted by their own questionable petard? The tennis girls said he was seen with the best-looking dates, and rarely the same one more than twice in a row—almost as if the variety were deliberate. Now really. If he was going to be that way, he could at least have been a Democrat. He turned after Albert's introduction, took my hand, and looked into the furthest reaches of my eyes. Wow. He had my vote.

"So you're Dr. Beckmann's beautiful wife," he smiled smoothly. "It must keep you on your toes, being married to such a brilliant man."

Oh good grief, what a patronizing comment. Was it possible our head of state was not the sharpest knife in the drawer? I refused to answer. Albert stepped in before the silence could become awkward. "She manages pretty well, actually."

The governor chuckled and threw a quick glance toward the door to check any incoming guests. Apparently, no one seemed more promising so he turned back to us. Then his mood turned pensive. "I don't know what I'm going to do without Jann," he said, and for the moment I thought he was speaking a rare, unvarnished truth. "She ran me like a sports car, told me where to be when, reminded me when I needed a tune-up." He looked up. "One of the first things I did after getting elected was steal her from Johnson and Wray. Lovely girl, wasn't she? Striking. And you could trust her absolutely. Loyal, you know? I never wondered if she was writing some tell-all book on the side." He shook his large, beautiful head. "This is all very hard to believe."

I wanted to elicit a few more thoughts on the recently deceased from her former employer but an elderly woman came up to ask about a pending piece of legislation. Short of sending her careening into the caviar, there was nothing for it. Outmanuevered by a sweet old thing with a pet peeve. Darn. We wandered off, heading toward a window to admire the view. "How do you know him so well?" I asked Albert.

"I was called in to advise him about some health bills that were coming up for his signature. That was only a couple of months ago, so he hasn't had a chance to forget me yet." Albert glanced back at the gov, who was trying to extricate himself from the intense lady. "Suave, isn't he? Anyway, most of the time. And so different from Parker. I wonder what it was like for Jann, coming home after a day with that guy."

LeMay, who had been talking and accepting condolences from small groups of guests, must have sensed us using his name. His chin rose suddenly, like that of an animal hearing the cocking of a rifle. He separated himself from a rather dowdy looking couple and came over, joining us at the huge window. "This is so weird," he said confidingly. "I mean, some of these people I've scarcely met. They're Jann's friends." Never mind that we, Albert and I, weren't exactly his inseparable buddies either. "Of course, she was always close with the whole Vietnamese community. They liked to get together and speak the language, talk about the old days. Which pretty well left me out. Not the language, of course, but—" He broke off as the sun found a glass building across the way and sent a reflecting beam straight into the room, dazzling us. "Quite a view, isn't it?" he said with pride, using an arm to encompass the whole of it. "That's what made Jann want this place so much in spite of the shape it was in."

I looked again. Who could blame her? The sweeps of mountain to the south and west were lovely, still snow-capped and majestic. Below, the city knelt at their feet and worshiped. Beautiful and, for Jann, deadly. Without those craggy peaks, she could have survived, guiding the impaired plane to a safe landing on flat ground. Did the murderer really know *Sweet Juliet* would be in those deadly mountains when the engine failed? What made him (or her) think Jann wasn't heading for the flatlands? Where would we have been had we started toward Devil's Tower?

"How did she ever have time to furnish it so beautifully?" I asked, anxious to think of other things. "She was so busy."

Parker smiled, looking around appreciatively at his own digs. "You should have seen it when we took it over. It was unbelievable. Seventy years of imbedded industrial filth. I thought she was nuts, but Jann had this...vision. And she was unstoppable, really." He looked away, the suffering again reflected in his face. "When she knew what she wanted, no obstacle was too great. If she hadn't had that ferocious will, she'd still be in Saigon." He was staring out the window, seeing who knew what unspeakable scenes. I wondered if it occurred to him that, had she stayed, she might still be alive. He resumed his host mode. "Anyway, so good of you to come. Can I have LaShawn bring you something to drink? LaShawn..." He called to the young woman, the one we'd seen earlier with the flawless tiny braids. She was working in the kitchen area, a space without doors completely open to the main room. She spun smartly on her heels and headed over.

Her eyes were still red-rimmed though her demeanor was completely professional. She couldn't have been very old, in her mid-twenties at most, not yet jaded enough to forget the tragedy behind this party. Here was one person besides our host who seemed to feel some deep loss. I'd seen her at the service, crying quietly and steadily into a handkerchief. Parker must have found her grief disconcerting. He tried for some small talk. "LaShawn has been with us for, what, eight years?" he asked, looking to her at last for a confirmation she refused to give. Then to cover the silence, he added, "She and Jann were real friends. She'll get you a drink. I'd do it, but, um, yeah…those folks…" His speech was beginning to assume that herky-jerky affect that made him seem so ill at ease in company. He gave LaShawn a pat on the shoulder, watched her stiffen, and hurried off to some departing guests. We asked for gin and tonics though summer was just a memory and she left to oblige, managing the transaction without once meeting our eyes. I underlined my previous decision to chat with this lady before too long.

Drinks eventually in hand, we started toward the dining room table for want of anything else to do.

"Look, there's Ozzie Westgaard," said Albert, gesturing with a celery stick. He bit into it with a crunch. "Wonder why he's here."

"Ozzie as in…?"

"Oswald. He's one of the legal team for the school." Medical schools, in a litigious age, needed all the legal help they could get. "I've worked with him, remember? That conflict of interest case with one of our researchers?" He swallowed the stringy snack and headed in the man's direction. Having nothing better to do, I followed.

Westgaard was one of the three-piece suits I'd noticed earlier, a roundish man of average height, late fifties maybe, with thick white hair that gleamed. The waves, combed back, reflected light. He broke away from a small group and met Albert halfway.

"Dr. Beckmann. Nice to see you."

"And you, sir." Albert occasionally loved formality. "This is my wife, Grace."

"Mrs. Beckmann. A pleasure."

I nodded, silent.

"So how are you, Ozzie?"

"Fine, fine. Shocked, of course, at all this." He gestured vaguely around. "Seems to me Parker once said you owned that plane with him."

"Right." Albert looked for and found a cocktail napkin. "If we ever find out who caused this tragedy, there might even be a lawsuit in it. Particularly if it was some idiot's careless mistake, someone who worked on the plane."

Westgaard looked down, modestly. "I'm here if you need me."

"Thanks, Oz." Albert, finding no obvious place for the crumpled napkin, tucked it in his pocket. "Say, how do you know LeMay?"

"Met through the hospital." He was quiet a moment as if deciding whether to go on. No one jumped in to help. "We've had some...um, dealings together," he said finally. "I think he's got a good product. In fact, I'm one of his major investors, and not just for my clients either. Have a nice piece of the action myself." He pulled an ostentatious gold pocket watch from its housing in his vest and made a point of checking it. "Oops, better be going."

After a few obligatory niceties, Ozzie Westgaard headed for the door, stopping only to say a few words to Parker. For a man with rather short legs, he seemed to be moving fast.

We looked around. No one looked familiar. A few

people appeared more than passably interesting but there was no obvious way to approach them. Albert was starting to consult his watch, a more pedestrian wrist model. He'd been good for too long. Home for the hunter.

I was about to give in. I took one more artichoke bottom from the diminishing supply and, knowing it was my last, was about to enjoy it when a burst of angry, loud voices stopped me. Every head in the room turned suddenly.

LeMay was arguing in a language I couldn't understand. Matching his anger, arms flying in violent arcs, was a young Asian woman. Well, maybe, on second look, not all that young. Mid-thirties, perhaps. He was shouting, she was screaming, and they looked like the only thing keeping the argument from turning physical was the roomful of people. Parker's face had turned from white to red, his incomprehensible words jumping around erratically. The woman, dressed in a short, tight purple skirt, was doing everything but paw the ground. Since I hadn't noticed who started what, I couldn't tell exactly who was on the offense.

Did the woman look like a shorter, stockier version of Jann or was that my imagination, a Caucasian's inability to analyze Asian features? Certainly she didn't dress like Jann, who would never, I was fairly sure, be caught dead in anything so overtly seductive.

Before the guests had a chance to react or intervene, it ended abruptly. The strength seemed to leave the woman's body and, with a stricken look, she turned and dragged herself through the door, her back bent like an old woman's under a heavy load.

The sudden silence made it obvious that everyone in the room had been listening. Parker looked up, clearly embarrassed, shrugged his shoulders in a halfhearted apology, and headed for the area in the kitchen where the liquor bottles were arrayed. His lips still moved. In his head the argument still raged. Ice clinked into a glass. The guests, a little rattled, restarted their conversations.

"Who in the world was that?"

"Mailin Duong, I think. Jann's sister," the man next to me offered.

So I was right about the resemblance. "Well," I said, half expecting her to charge again through the door, and maybe with a gun. "I wouldn't want to see her when she was *really* mad."

SIX

THE MAN'S expression could have been classified as a smile. I hadn't noticed him in the loft earlier. Maybe he'd just arrived. He held out a nicely manicured hand to Albert. "Hello," he said to Albert. "I'm Nicholas Qualls."

"Albert Beckmann."

"Hello," I offered. "Grace Beckmann."

Nicholas Qualls nodded. He looked vaguely Mediterranean, possibly Greek, about five ten with curly dark hair and a tan that might have developed its luster on a beach in Crete. Under the Brioni jacket, all sorts of undulating, gym-polished muscles suggested themselves. I decided not to offer a hand. Considering the guy's primo physical condition, I figured my delicate bones might be at risk.

"Known LeMay long?" he asked.

Albert began explaining our connections to the bereaved. Qualls may have assumed we knew more than we did about Parker's life. If so, he soon learned how wrong he was. Co-owning a plane makes for a pretty loose confederation. I amused myself by staring at the man's eyes, which were compelling and deep, a dark brown tinged with red, odd, like cordovan shoes.

Finally, he must have realized it was his turn. He put down a tall glass of something and wiped the

moisture from his hands. "I own Bio-Quest Pharmaceuticals," he said. "I'm in the process of buying
LeMay out, as a matter of fact. That is, if everything
checks out the way we think it will." His voice was
deep, authoritative almost to the point of arrogance,
but it carried a slight inflection, an element of
"street." Albert would later say that only I could
hear that. "We're about to transition from research
and development to manufacture and distribution,"
he continued. "We've also raised fifteen million for
additional research through a limited partnership."
He sounded like a training film. "Our main office
is actually in Kansas City," he added, "and that's
where I live, but we keep an apartment here because
of all the action in pharmaceuticals around this
town. Since you're a doctor, you probably know
about the stuff that's going on."

"Not as much as I should," said Albert, perking
up. He liked talking shop. "I'm not even absolutely
sure what Parker makes in his laboratories."

Qualls frowned, remembering. "Isotope tracers.
Artificial breast milk. An experimental NSAID that
the FDA hasn't signed off on yet. Those are the
main things his people are working on. Products that
fit our own mix."

"I assume you'd close up this place and move the
research to your home office." Albert sounded casual but I could see the wheels turning. He wouldn't
have to worry about sharing another plane with Parker if Parker moved away.

"Maybe. Maybe not. That's up to LeMay. If the
sale goes through and he wants to hang in, to keep

his lab here and just act as director, I won't object. He has that option. If not..." He brushed some imaginary lint from a sleeve. "Since I was in town," he went on, "and this bad thing happened with his wife, thought the decent thing to do was stop in and pay my respects. Not political, though, you know? Nothing about the deal. It's going through." He looked up, caught by an idea. "Any interest in doing a little clinical testing?"

Albert took a step back. "Um, sorry. I don't think that would be possible."

Perceiving a rebuff, Qualls lost interest in us. "Have to be going now. Busy. Nice to meet you." He glanced behind him at two men standing against a collection of chrome shelving in one corner, saying nothing, watching everything. They met his eye and the older man nodded slightly. He was holding his left arm stiffly, hand wedged in a pocket as if it might fall without the support. A war injury? The younger of the two, a big guy, had turned away from us, leaving only the impression of long, oily hair. They all began moving toward the door. His goons, I thought, and then canceled the idea as melodramatic. Qualls nodded across the room to Parker and he and his men left the condo in quasi-formation.

The crowd was thinning. I gave Albert a barely perceptible time-to-leave sign which he acknowledged with relief. I wondered if he had become as uncomfortable as I had. Everything about those in this room seemed vaguely artificial. People acting and overacting. There was Jann's sister Mailin, screaming publicly at Parker. Certainly inappropriate, during what should have been at least a mildly funereal gathering. LaShawn with her cornrows, weeping for her late employer and flinching from Parker's touch. The governor of our fair state, coming himself not only to the service but to this gathering, and then hanging around. Waiting for something? Or somebody?

And Qualls. I needed to think about him, maybe in a good hot bubble bath laced with oils. One idea had come through all the hot air. Qualls was lying about the deal being in the bag. And he was lying about not needing Parker. And what was a successful businessman doing traveling with what sure as heck looked like bodyguards? Was he Warren Buffett or the Godfather?

And last, where was Hallie? Hallie of the seductive telephone answering message, Hallie whose number Parker had gone to such trouble to hide. Had she been at the service? I didn't think so. But she wasn't here now, I was pretty sure of that. Voices can lie, but the seven women left in the room looked like no-nonsense career types in their early fall suits and silk shells. Not the seductive message ilk. Time to split before I lost what was left of my mind.

The trip home from the caverns of lower downtown brought us back to more immediate concerns. Our boys. Our sabbatical-to-be, the foreign one. Our work. I was researching a long piece about reservation politics as it played out in one of the country's poorest Native American tribes. The fun thing about it was that the tribe wasn't going to be poor for long. It was sitting on some serious natural resources, enough to make this group of more or less defeated people forget their hot and dusty corner of the world and, for the first time, think big thoughts. The leftish magazine that had okayed the query was never in much of a hurry, so I had the luxury of time. Of course, if I'd needed the freelance money, I would have had time constraints of a different kind, but the fact was I didn't.

"I do hope my Indian stuff will be terrific," I said, apropos of nothing. "I need that magazine to publish whatever articles come out of your sabbatical."

Albert was eyeing a car in front of us, full of kids and beer cans. "You'll do fine," he said absently.

The trouble I could foresee with the Native American article was going to be the elusive nature of the truth. All truths seemed to be elusive these days.

And, of course, I was always worried about the twins. Or, to be a bit more exact, I was always worried about Spence.

Supper was simmering when we arrived home, and it smelled terrific. I didn't have the heart to tell Millie that her best lamb stew would be served to two people who had eaten their way through an elegant afternoon buffet. The boys, who inhaled whatever Millie cooked, would more than make up for our lack of appetite. I asked her, when she took a break from sautéing the onions, what had happened since we left.

Millie lived vicariously through our varied doings, so we got an elaborate rundown on the day's calls. She chatted happily to anyone who phoned when we were out. She was even up-to-date on the marital problems of a young postdoc in Albert's department, one who had tried to leave a simple message about a meeting change. No one escaped Millie.

"And Paul's in his room, curled up with some kind of how-to test book. He also has the radio blaring, but he says it doesn't hurt his concentration." She gave the onions a disapproving swish with a spatula. "It's his ears I'm worried about."

"And Spence?"

"Out."

"Great. Terrific. At least one of them will make it to college."

I waited till we reached the great room before exploding to Albert. "And you wonder why I worry about that kid." This was our favorite room in the house, the place we all repaired to after a hard day. Couches and chairs were comfortable and copious. Everyone could slouch. A Herez on the floor hid all small stains and even forgave some large ones. Tables and ledges and bookcases absorbed clutter without looking unduly messy. Traditionally, we talked in this room.

The father of my children was going through the mail that Millie had piled neatly by the bar. "You love worrying about him. You prefer reprobates. It's Paul I worry about, the fact that nothing he does can excite you. He just can't win you over."

"Paul is fine. He's wonderful. Of course I love him. His teachers love him. He has friends. My mother worships him. Paul does not need my constant approbation."

Albert cut his finger on an envelope, winced, and sucked the blood. "Darn." He found a tissue in his pocket and stuck it to the wound. "Okay, so not your constant approbation," he said, watching the growing spot of red with a distant interest. "But how about some small notice that he's doing a terrific job of living? I mean, he has to have some feeling that he's number two with you. You're going to make him a candidate for therapy in about thirty years."

"He'll be able to afford it. Spence will be digging ditches somewhere." I straightened a pile of books defensively. "Oh, I suppose I may be a little biased. I tend to root for the underdog. Somewhere down deep, Paul understands that." I kicked off my memorial service shoes—soft, funky ones but still not as comfortable as bare feet. "I can just imagine what's going to happen with these PSATs. And here it's *Paul* who's studying. Can you believe it?"

Albert flipped on the television, an obnoxious huge-screen jobbie that he loved and I found embarrassing. The late-afternoon news—network, not local—was winding down with its soft feature. And there was a plane, so big on that huge screen it felt like it had dropped directly into our house. A private plane, someone's favorite toy, crashed on a city street. The announcer's voice was talking about the hazards of small planes flying over residential areas. I closed my eyes and felt like I was in *Sweet Juliet* again, circling the city, spotting familiar buildings that looked so angular and sparse from above. There had been moments in the last few days, admittedly not many, when I actually missed the idea of flying. I mean real flying, in a tiny plane. The crash was less than half a week old. It happened Friday and it was now only Monday, but I had a strangely sad feeling when I pictured the empty spot in our old hangar. Albert must have been feeling it, too, watching that story. I was actually sinking into nostalgia but it didn't last long.

Albert's arms were draped across the back of the leather couch. He talked without taking his eyes from the set. "When you're all done spoiling Spence and making a neurotic of Paul, how would you like to go out with me to the airport again and start looking for another plane?"

I poured a tonic water over ice for myself at the bar, squeezing in two lime quarters Millie had left for me. Then I splashed some pepper vodka into another glass and took both over to the couch, handing Albert his spicy drink. I sank down beside him and propped my bare feet on the coffee table. "You just can't stand the idea that we haven't killed ourselves yet, huh? We need another plane."

"Sure we do. I do."

I sighed. "Isn't there some productive work you're supposed to be doing?"

"Have you any idea how much pointless research is done in the name of medicine? The world will not stop turning if I never get this stuff done."

"But you will get it done and done beautifully. And the world will be a better place. I know my boy-o." I ran my hand down his leg. His arm, the one that had perched on the back of the couch, dropped down around me. Did funerals make us feel affectionate?

"Whoops. Think I'll go out and come back in again." Paul, his arms full of oversized paperbacks, was standing in the doorway. Albert's arm swung back to his lap.

"Great timing, kid," he said. "Can't let these old folks have any fun."

Paul, his black vest, shirt, and jeans blending into the background and reducing him to nothing but a face, wasn't embarrassed. He'd caught us at worse. "Have you seen Spence?"

I took my bare feet from the coffee table and crossed my legs discreetly. Children are such a pain when they keep us from behaving like they do. "Millie just said he went out. Didn't he tell you where he was going?"

"Not really." He fell into an overstuffed chair and checked the television to see if we had tuned in anything interesting. We hadn't. "He's so lucky. He's going to cool all this PSAT stuff without cracking a book. I wish I could do that."

"Excuse me?" I looked with amazement at Mr. Achievement.

"What?"

"For heaven's sake, Paul, you're the one who gets good grades, not Spence. You've been running circles around him since first grade."

"Grades are different. You can work for grades.

These tests measure smarts. You watch, Mom. Spence'll cool 'em. He's a genius, like Dad.''

I turned away, hiding my expression of surprise. When had Paul started considering himself the weaker of the pair? The weird thing was that Spence considered himself an also-ran too. Wasn't it just a couple days ago that he'd assured us how well Paul would do on the tests? He'd told me before how Paul intimidated him in a classroom, made him feel like a hopeless buffoon. Being a twin must be terribly difficult. I didn't even know what it felt like to have a brother or sister.

As if reading my mind, he said, "You're so lucky, Mom. I really think it's much cooler to be an only child. Tyler's an only child." Tyler Oates was his best friend after Spence. "And your weird pal Parker LeMay once told me he was an only child. And that he liked it. He thought brothers and sisters were nothing but a major pain."

I thought of Mailin, Jann's sister, and the scene we had witnessed earlier in the afternoon. No wonder Parker disliked siblings, or anyway siblings-in-law. "When did you talk to Parker?" I asked.

"I ran into him at the hospital once when we were meeting Dad. He was there on some kind of drug business. Dad introduced us. Kind of a spook, I thought. Seemed sort of nervous all the time. But he was really nice about our being twins and all. He said that sometimes when people are married to each other, they kind of become like twins. Think of the same things at the same time. Start to reach for the same magazine together. You know. Do you suppose he was talking about himself?''

"I wouldn't be surprised.''

"Then that's really too bad. That his wife's dead. He'll never have anyone who understands him quite like that again.'' He grabbed a handful of rice crackers from a bowl on the side table and sank into a study of the television section, searching for some less adult diversion.

I couldn't let that idea go by so easily. I turned to Albert, who had switched to "Headline News" for the ball scores. "Do we have that close a relationship? Have we bonded like that?''

"Nope. We've always been two people.''

"Maybe Jann and Parker were so close because of their background. Maybe that happened when he took her out of Vietnam as a young girl.'' For years, she must have had nowhere else to turn for support. And he must have felt enormous responsibility, removing her from family and country and language.

Eventually, I thought, this ambitious, smart woman did find a life in America. I wondered if that would have bothered Parker. Would he have been proud or threatened? And would she have come to resent their closeness as claustrophobic? Was she attracted to her governor/boss?

"Do you suppose Parker was having an affair with Hallie, whoever she is?'' I was half talking to myself. "Do you think he could have killed Jann?''

"Maybe.'' Albert yawned hugely. "He could have done it. Husbands are certainly the first the police look at when a woman dies violently.''

He was right there, of course, but in this case, I could as soon imagine Parker killing Jann as I could his cutting off his own arm. They were obviously soulmates, as much twins as our own two boys.

Clearly, we, my reluctant husband and I, had a lot to do. I started making a mental list of people to interview. This was going to be where my writing career provided the best cover possible. I'd tell people I was working on a story. A story about war brides? A story about the dangers of flying small planes? A story about the pharmaceutical industry? Choose one. I could fit the subject to the interview. But I'd better keep my stories straight, once I started. There was a possible murderer out there and this was no game. Someone seemed to be playing for keeps.

SEVEN

I WAS SO ANXIOUS to get to my Tuesday morning doubles game, I didn't even react when the phone rang at seven-ten. Albert got it, fielded it, and hung up.

"The police," he informed me groggily. "They want to talk to us. Today. I suggested they come at eleven-thirty. You'll be back by then, won't you?"

I nodded, pulling on a long-sleeved T-neck and sweats. I hoped cops didn't grade down for sloppiness. Fortunately, our tennis club didn't have a strong dress code. We played outdoors as far into the winter as possible, which meant we'd turn out for anything above forty degrees, even if it required jackets and gloves. At this point halfway through October, just a couple of weeks before we fell back from Daylight Savings Time, we woke in the cold and dark, and the idea of tennis seemed remote.

But it wasn't the fun and exercise that drew me today. I needed to touch base with the girls. This wasn't just any tennis foursome. This was a parliament of mavens.

The maven of mavens was Beebee Ballard. Beebee didn't work, technically speaking. Her sweetly aging mother had moved in with her; multitudes of Ballard children, supposedly in colleges around the area, always seemed to be home for lunch; and the whole complicated household would have fallen into chaos without her ready presence. What Beebee knew besides earth-mothering, however, was money. Her stockbroker husband called home often. She had a fax and computer right in her enormous kitchen and an old master's degree in economics yellowing in the back bedroom. She also had a bullet serve she could place right on the T that was a killer to return from the deuce court. Ever noticed how lethal tennis talk sounds? I arrived at the clubhouse fifteen minutes early in the hopes of catching a moment alone with her and wasn't disappointed. She was there. Playing tennis was as close as she could get to running away from home, and she wasn't likely to miss a second, even if it would have meant being so cold she had to play in a ski suit.

Beebee, ever intrepid, was in shorts. A competitive athlete in her youth, the experience translated now into a look that was both solid and somehow trustworthy. Capable. At forty-six, her legs were still muscular and firm. If the waist had gone a bit soft, nothing else had. She was on me before I'd closed the sliding door.

"Oh, Grace, I couldn't wait to see you. A murder! I mean, the papers haven't come right out and said it, but obviously that's what they think. Talk to me, talk to me."

I sat beside her on the rump-sprung old couch and checked discreetly for eavesdroppers. The girl who ran the front desk was out of range. The club pro, busy as a plugged-in ball machine during the season, was walking slowly and absently through to his office. I waited for him to disappear from the deserted lobby.

"Okay," I said. "But first, you've got to tell me everything you know about Parker LeMay's pharmaceutical company. And about another one called Bio-Quest. In fact, I could use anything you know about the pharmaceutical business in general. I haven't had a chance to do my homework."

"In five minutes or less?"

"We have fifteen. Or more. That's plenty. Sarah Jane will show up but then she'll have to go to the bathroom and read the bulletin boards and sign up for something. You know. And Magda...well, forget Magda."

Magda, our adorable Magda, was never less than twenty minutes late for the game. People who saw us waiting for her week after week asked how we resisted lynching her. Our stock response: we left the rope in our other purse. Today, her little aberration fit into my plans perfectly. I wanted answers even more than I wanted tennis.

"Well, the pharmaceutical industry in general, gee, only about the most profitable industry in the country." Beebee quickly warmed to her subject. "We're talking billions. You're a doctor's wife, you know the big names." She raised her eyes, as if reading the companies from some elevated ticker tape. "Abbott. Novartis. Hoffman-LaRoche. Pfizer. Ely Lilly and Company. Lederle. Parke-Davis. Should I go on? Check the Manufacturers' Association in Washington. Are you researching an article?"

"How can you just run this stuff off? Does your husband talk in his sleep?"

She blushed slightly, her already high-color cheeks going deeper red. "Let's just say we work together on occasion." She swung around on the lumpy couch, tucking both legs under her, so she could face me. "Let's see, what else did you ask? Bio-Quest? Don't know, but let me see what I can turn up. As for Parker LeMay...oh." She grinned wryly. "This isn't for an article, is it. What are you doing, turning sleuth?"

"Trying. All I know about Parker's firm is that he manufactures, um, radioactive tracers, something about artificial breast milk, I think, and...oh yeah, nonsteroidals."

"Good products. Very competitive. How can a small company go head-to-head with the biggies on things like that?"

"Why not?"

"All kinds of costs. Huge ones. Distribution, hot waste disposal, advertising. You can't believe how much the big drug companies spend on ads, R & D, clinical testing. And approval processes."

"And parties. And symposia. Sure I can. I see it all the time. But still, the world seems to be full of start-up companies with a product or two."

I felt a gust of cool air as the door to the club-house opened. "Hey, close that thing."

"I am, I am." Sarah Jane, in hot-pink warm-ups and matching flowered shirt, breezed in, belatedly slamming the door behind her. "Hi, guys. I see that three of us are on time. Be right back. Have to make a pit stop." She was off to the back of the clubhouse and the locker rooms.

We waved at her departing figure. "Okay." I turned back to Beebee who was starting to collect her racquet case and balls. I knew time was running out. "Have you heard anything about a buyout of Parker LeMay's firm? Hostile or otherwise? In fact, do you know anything at all about how well he does? I really can't tell by the way they live, or lived. Their downtown loft is beautiful, but I think they bought it for a song. He, of course, owns half of what used to be our plane but otherwise, no clue. Cars, clothes, you know, nothing special. He could be paying off massive loans. You'd think the bottom line would be healthy if someone wants to buy him out."

"Well, for sure if the buyout is hostile. Then you look for underlying and usually unrealized value. But not necessarily if we're talking merger. LeMay could have something another company wants. Gracie, my love, you are asking too much of me." Beebee ran her hand through a nest of curls. "I know that the word was he was going in the tank, but that was a couple of years ago. He obviously survived. Possibly thrived. In fact, he must have. His stock trades over the counter, so he did well enough to take it public recently. That requires capital."

We could hear a flush and then voices in the distance. Sarah Jane flirting with the pro. I hurried on. "Can you get some details for me?"

"Sure," she said. "Try, anyway." We gathered our stuff and headed out the door.

The day was by now definitely shaping up as a
perfect specimen of glorious mid-autumn. Wind
screens on all the courts had been removed, allowing
us to enjoy the colors of some ancient oaks surrounding the club. A foursome of retired men oc-
cupied one of the lower courts, but otherwise we
had the place pretty much to ourselves and we liked
it that way. Still, I was getting very antsy by the
time Magda arrived. The three of us had been warming up on the court for fifteen minutes. Sometimes
she was so late, we ended up drafting a stray fourth
or playing Canadian. She had long since stopped
apologizing or coming up with fresh excuses. What
is, is.

"Gracie," she yelled, closing the gate behind her
and running over to hug me. "My phone has been
ringing off the hook about you. You are so lucky to
be *alive!* What a terrible thing! Come over while I
change my shoes and tell me all about it."

The three of us wandered over near the courtside
bench to stand around while Magda completed her
toilette. A style of maximum drama added zest to
all her proceedings. "Do you suppose the governor
was behind it?" she asked. "I mean, Jann LeMay
was his right-hand person. She was a lot more than
just his press liaison. Maybe they were involved
with each other and he had to get rid of her! Maybe
it was blackmail!" She looked up into three dubious
faces. "Well, I mean, it *could* be. Everyone knows
he dates a lot of girls. But Jann was married. That
could have caused a scandal."

"You really think so?" I pretended all this was new to keep her going.

"Well, yeah." She finished tying the last shoe and began fishing around for sunblock even though the sun was so low in the sky, it couldn't have brought out a freckle. Care of her skin was more second nature than any particular vanity. Magda had an easy beauty and wonderful coloring and seemed unaware of both. "Wasn't there a rumor a few months ago that the press had caught up with him at the apartment of some woman and that he denied it? I mean, he was really irate, for some reason."

What had I heard? "Wasn't that just something in the underground weekly? Of course, I'm not part of that political universe, but I didn't think it was anything much. One of the usual rumors power players have to contend with."

Magda shrugged, her eyebrows expressive. "Listen, Jann LeMay was a lovely woman. I've seen her picture once or twice, in the paper or on television. She and the gov were inseparable, they say. He wouldn't be the first man to fall for one of these high-powered career gals he works with every day. I mean, weirder things have happened."

I bounced a tennis ball on my racquet and remembered my meeting with the handsome Honorable One yesterday. At the time, I'd felt that Parker couldn't possibly compete in either looks or savoir faire with this man. Had Jann been caught between them? As Magda said, weirder things have happened.

Concentration is the hallmark of champions, no

matter the game, which may explain why I couldn't hit the broad side of the clubhouse that day. I double-faulted three times and spanked a dozen returns into the net. The sun was more of an issue at this time of year, but even I wasn't liar enough to blame it for my problems. I play tennis to forget everyday concerns, but wow, not today. My mind was racing around drug companies with billion-dollar businesses and governors perhaps involved romantically with a member of their staff. Once, I raised the racquet to serve and thought I saw *Sweet Juliet* flying overhead. Besides, I had one eye on my watch. The police were showing up at our house at eleven-thirty. It was Lose With Gracie day.

The game ended finally and not a moment too soon. Beebee caught up with me on the way out, taking my arm conspiratorially. "I'll get back to you tomorrow. Thursday for sure. I'll have Dick dig around, and I'll see what the computer turns up. We can access the Net as easily at home as at the office." Then, with a quick look at Magda, who was too far away to hear, she added, "Too bad there's no Web site dedicated to extramarital affairs among the rich and famous. I could check out the gov while I'm on-line."

I laughed, waved good-bye, found the Aurora, and started home. Men didn't know what friendship was, I thought for the thousandth time as I waited at the one busy corner for the light to change. For one thing, they never knew how to ask each other for help. That would smack of weakness and violate some Iron John kind of thing. Certainly Beebee was in a better position than I to research the financial questions surrounding Parker's business, and I knew that deep down she was pleased to be asked. Men loved being asked for help. They just couldn't be the askee. And then there was the place of gossip. Did men gossip? By the time Albert told me a juicy item, it had already run in the morning paper. Women could nose out a story. Their instincts were in place. Of course, all that was going on was acute observation, seeing or hearing the little things.

Whatever, they had what I needed now. Scuttle-butt. Gossip. Hearsay. The smoke that could lead me to a fire.

EIGHT

A STRANGE, DARK CAR was parked on the circular drive when I got home. I went in from the garage through the kitchen, where Millie was doing creative things with leftovers for lunch. Talk radio was on but the volume uncharacteristically low. I smelled cut pineapple. Millie gave me a meaningful look.

"They've been here about fifteen minutes. And they're not in uniform. I thought all policemen wore uniforms. Should I ask if they want a cup of coffee?" Correct police etiquette was not part of her experience.

"I'll do it. I'm not late. They must have come early. Is Albert nervous?"

She tucked a strand of fine hair behind her ear. "You know how he looks at his watch a lot when he'd rather be someplace else? I think he'd rather be someplace else." Have I mentioned lately that Millie doesn't miss a trick?

Everyone rose when I walked in the great room, gentlemen all.

"Gracie, meet Detectives Morrisey and Munz. Gentlemen, my wife, Grace."

Morrisey was clearly the alpha male, a small, compact man with graying hair and an aura of being in charge. His reserved, almost courtly manner blew all my pop culture conceptions of police detectives out the window. "We were early," he apologized. "Hope our coming ahead of schedule hasn't caused you any inconvenience."

"Not at all, and please do sit down. Can I get either of you some coffee?"

They returned to their seats. "Thanks, no. We had plenty down at the station." Morrisey did all the talking. Munz, tall, broad, and deferential, seemed to know his place. After a muttered "Good morning," I never heard another word from him.

"The detectives are working with the federal government on this case," Albert explained as everyone sat back down. He had dressed in chinos and a cotton shirt with sleeves rolled to the elbow, as casual as he ever got. "They're looking for anything we might have noticed that was unusual around the airport or the plane. And anything we might have to add about the LeMays themselves, and Jann in particular." He sat back in his favorite chair and toyed with a pencil. Now that I was back, he could relax a bit and let me run with the ball. "I told them what Potts said about Jann's odd behavior at takeoff, about her operating what seemed like a rogue airplane, not communicating with the tower."

"We'd be interested in any impressions you might have about that day, Mrs. Beckmann," said Morrisey quietly. "Or about any other time in the last few days."

"Well...okay." I thought a minute. "Did my husband mention that empty container that was found on the plane after it crashed? Parker LeMay didn't seem to make a big deal of it when he saw it. It was about so big." I held my hands apart five or six inches. "And round. Opened in half."

Morrisey answered. "We heard about it. We're checking it out."

Something clicked. They knew but weren't saying. I kept going. "Did Albert tell you about the phone number we saw Parker remove from Jann's wallet? Or about the bad blood that seems to exist between him and Jann's sister?"

Munz brought a fresh pen out from the inside pocket of his sportcoat and started writing furiously. Morrisey seemed to come awake. He leaned forward, his shoe catching in the fringe of the Herez. "What about this phone number? No, we haven't heard about that."

Albert shook his head, embarrassed. "My wife gets a bit nosy sometimes."

"Parker slipped it out of Jann's wallet and put it in his pocket." I recited the number, still firmly in my head. "I, sort of, found a way to see it. It was written on a piece of memo paper from the governor's office. And that's all it was, just that number."

"Did you try to call it?" Morrisey was looking at me with a pointed, somehow knowing expression.

"Of course."

He smiled. "And, of course, we'll call it, too. What did you discover?"

"Someone named Hallie. An answering machine. Sexy voice. I haven't tried since. Maybe Parker was having a fling and Jann had found out. Was carrying her number around."

Now Albert was looking at me, too, his eyes deliberately wide. "If I decide to have an affair, are you going to carry my mistress's phone number around with you?"

"It won't be necessary," I replied sweetly. "She's as good as dead the minute I find out, so her phone will be disconnected."

The detectives grinned. Munz continued to write.

"Was there an autopsy, do you know?" I asked. "Maybe Jann's weird behavior during takeoff was caused by drugs of some kind."

"We thought of that," said Morrisey. "Apparently, LeMay had the body cremated as soon as it was released. However, as you know, it wasn't pilot error that caused the crash, so the question of drugs is pretty incidental." His lips tightened. "I would have liked to have had her chemistries, though."

He took out his own pad now, though Munz was still busily taking notes. "Now, I'm afraid I have to ask you about your whereabouts on Thursday night."

We both looked up surprised, and perhaps a bit affronted. Albert answered first. "Do you think we destroyed the engine of our own plane?"

Morrisey managed a thin smile. "Actually, no. But it's a routine question."

"Why Thursday night?" I asked. "Albert hadn't been in that plane for five days." I looked to him for confirmation. "You took it up a week ago Sunday, remember?" Morrisey was listening hard, so hard he'd stopped writing. "The plane probably hadn't been flown since then," I explained to the detective. "So the sabotage could have happened just about any time."

Morrisey was almost embarrassed to have to contradict me. He couldn't meet my eye. "Not really, Mrs. Beckmann. Apparently, it had flown. Mr. Potts said Parker LeMay had given the okay for a charter operator you both know to take it Thursday morning for a short delivery. So we know it was okay as of about eight o'clock Thursday night when he closed his flight plan."

This was news. That left only a twelve-hour hole during which the plane could have been tampered with.

"Yeah," Albert said with a nod, "we've done that now and then. As a favor. Let one of the airport regulars borrow the plane."

"So," said Morrisey, "we have a time frame. Is the hangar usually locked at night? Potts says he's faithful about it."

"He's very reliable," agreed Albert. "But he wouldn't have been there at eight at night. Even he gets hungry enough to go home now and then. Who knows if the charter guy remembered to lock up?"

Munz and Morrisey were both quiet now, sitting straight, waiting for the teasers to be over and the main feature to begin. I realized what we hadn't said.

"We were at a meeting at the boys' school till about ten," I told them. "Then we came home. All sorts of people saw us earlier. The twins were still up when we got home. They saw us, and so did Millie, our housekeeper."

Morrisey seemed satisfied and entered the information into his notebook. Munz duplicated the effort.

The detectives stayed a while longer, finally accepting the offer of coffee and a sandwich, but they seemed to know most of what we had to tell them. We were hardly first on their list. They'd already spoken to the airport personnel and to Jack Potts. Someone must have told them about the argument at Parker's loft.

Almost as an afterthought, Morrisey asked the question I'd been waiting for. "Have you any reason to believe this, um, event might have been aimed at you? Any recent enemies? Either of you?"

Albert and I exchanged glances. "Certainly we've been wondering that ourselves, Detective," he volunteered. "Neither of us can think of anyone who might be out to get us or, for that matter, anyone who's even angry about anything. I know that's not much help."

Morrisey examined his hands. "You know we have to ask. It's our opinion that you were not the intended victims, but it is, of course, possible that we're wrong."

Yes, I thought. *It's certainly possible.* Did they realize how easily it could have been us broken apart on that mountain floor? Now that I knew they'd written us off as the target, it was more important than ever that we take matters into our own hands.

Morrisey shook our hands at the door and gave both of us cards. "Here's my number. Please call if anything occurs to you. And if something unusual happens, even if it seems unrelated, I'd appreciate hearing about it. There's a great deal to this case we don't understand. The story may have completely ended with Jann LeMay's life." He faced each of us in turn. "And maybe it didn't." He left without a good-bye down the front steps. Munz followed after with a solemn farewell nod. The classic man of few words.

We closed the door behind them and looked at each other, vaguely shaken. "Let's eat and get out of here," said Albert, putting an arm around my shoulder. "I need a change of scene. I need to forget this whole business." We headed toward the back of the house. "And I need a new plane."

A new plane! All this was going on and he was dreaming about a new plane.

Okay, if he was going to the airport, I was going with him. I needed to go back to the place this all began.

NINE

I MADE A SECTION of the FBO's lounge my own personal space, turning off the always blaring television and propping my shoeless feet on the coffee table. I'd brought a stack of aging, unread magazines to catch up with and had them spread on the couch beside me. Too many magazines were occupational hazards of a freelancer. I always, as a gesture of thanksgiving, subscribed to any that were kind enough to publish my work. Then, of course, I was forced to read them.

Funny, really, that I'd ended up writing for magazines. We'd met over a magazine rack, Albert and I, at the Coop, me a bristly freshman, defensive about my western origins, and he to the East Coast manner born. He was leafing through an *Atlantic Monthly*. I was looking for *Rolling Stone*. I hazarded a quick look at him, so boyish with his uncut Seventies curls and long lashes, but made no move. I guessed our choice of reading material said it all.

I didn't think he'd noticed me till he cleared his throat and turned. "Can I help you find something?"

"Well...*Rolling Stone*, if you see it. If not, no big deal. I'll find one in the dorm." Still a little new at the game, I stuck out my hand. "Grace Spence."

"Albert Beckmann. Coffee?"

I didn't know anyone named Albert, unless you could count Queen Victoria's consort, but at least I wasn't naive enough to call him Al. The coffee was fine, good and strong. I never did read that month's *Rolling Stone*.

Maybe, if we solve Jann's murder, I should write a book. Magazines age like women, become invisible with time. Books age like men. They hang on a long while before losing their appeal.

Such musings were just beginning to make me drowsy when Albert returned, much cheered. He moved a stack of magazines to the floor and sat down in the space he'd cleared. "Would you believe there's another Turbo Arrow available? It's newer than *Sweet Juliet* was, and a little more expensive, but it has better avionics. And GPS."

"Can it be cured?"

"Global Positioning System. And a three-axis autopilot. We only had two before. Isn't that great?"

"My, yes. Great."

"You bet. These planes aren't being made at the moment, so they're getting really hard to find. This one's sitting at an airport in Ohio, but I saw the picture. You'd like it. It's very clean, very slick." He smiled at the memory of the three-by-five glossy. "Very beautiful."

I pulled my feet off the table, restoring their circulation, and slipped them back into their sneaks. "Just out of curiosity," I said, "why do you want the same plane that just killed your friend's wife? Are we into death wishes here?"

Albert stood, walked over to the coffeepot, and

poured himself a cup of hopeless sludge. It was mid-afternoon, and the pot had been on since seven or so. The FBO was very quiet at this hour. No one was behind the front desk. Sally and some man could be seen in Harley's office when they walked past the glass on the door. The line shack looked deserted. I hoped someone somewhere was listening to a scanner.

He came back with the cup. "I want a plane and I want one now, not next year. This one's available. I understand Turbo Arrows. I love Turbo Arrows. Any plane will crash if someone goes in and deliberately cuts its cables." He looked at me the way I once saw him look at a kindergarten teacher who suggested that Spence was just a little, tiny, wee bit difficult to handle. "Surely you're not blaming Sweet Juliet for that crash!"

"Surely not. And I do understand your withdrawal anxiety. It's been, what, five days since you lost your first plane?"

"I know. All right. Come on, unfoul your nest. Gather up this stuff and let's go to the old hangar. I want to talk to Jack Potts, see if he knows anything about this new plane. He seems to have a pretty good grapevine."

We drove over to *Sweet Juliet*'s old digs, even though it was an easy walk from the FBO. Easy, anyway, without forty pounds of magazines. Parking against the side wall created powerful emotions in both of us. Was it really just last Friday that we pulled up here, planning to take an innocent trip to

Devil's Tower? Somehow, it felt months had gone by.

Potts was working at an old, battered desk tucked in his office. He emerged, stopped to wash his hands, and then greeted us in his usual sober manner.

"How's it going, Doc? Mrs. B.?"

I waved in response and wandered away from the men. Maybe, though I guessed the police had looked, someone had missed something around the hangar's edges. I paced the periphery, checking for anything unusual. What had Jann done before leaving that morning? What path had she taken through the hangar? I felt her ghost around me. Unfortunately, any clue had apparently fallen victim to Jack Potts's broom.

Albert, meanwhile, exchanged the usual pleasantries before hurrying to the business at hand. "Wondered if you'd heard anything about the Turbo Arrow for sale in Ohio. Thought I'd check it out. Wouldn't commit to anything, of course, until you'd had a chance to look it over."

Potts glanced over to the empty space where *Sweet Juliet* once had parked. Albert looked, too, as if trying to adjust to the idea of another plane in that sacred spot. "Don't know anything about it, Doc. If you want, I'll ask around. Word has a way of getting out if the plane's a lemon."

"Thanks, Jack. I'd appreciate it."

"Planning to share it with LeMay again?"

"Funny, you know, I hadn't even thought of it," he lied. "No, I'll be buying this one alone. I guess

I just assumed Parker wouldn't want anything more to do with small planes. Why do you ask?''

Potts found some microscopic speck on the hangar floor to pick up and pocket. "Guess I'm just glad to hear that, is all."

Albert and I exchanged looks. Sensing a certain, what, hostility? Tension? I spoke up. "Sounds like you're trying to tell us something, Jack."

"Just that maybe he has a few enemies, is all."

"Parker?"

"Parker."

"Any one in particular?" asked Albert, now on alert.

"Oh...I don't know." Potts was looking uncomfortable. "Some guy, a couple days before the accident. Yelling at him. Real agitated."

I frowned, concentrating. "Had you seen him ever before?"

"Huh-uh," said Potts. "And too well-dressed to be flying that day, either. Three-piece outfit. Some sort of, like, paisley vest." He gestured across his stomach. "Looked a little, maybe..." He groped for the word. "Desperate. That's it. Desperate."

I'd seen a paisley vest, and recently, too. It came to me. "Your lawyer friend," I said to Albert. "At Parker's after the funeral. Remember? I'd thought it was a three-piece suit till he got closer. Pretty subtle pattern."

Albert thought a minute, then nodded. "Westgaard. Ozzie Westgaard. I noticed the vest. But I didn't find it subtle."

"Yeah, Oz or something," agreed Potts. "That's

what Parker called him. Big trouble there, I'd say.
And," he added, suddenly subdued, "there's others."

I was finally, as they say, in the moment. "Jack.
What?"

He looked at both of us with an unusual deliber-
ation. "Do you folks have a few minutes to spare?
I'd really like to talk to you about something.
'Specially you, Doc."

"Of course," I said quickly, before Albert could
take a quick peek at his watch.

We were ushered into the little hangar office, a
marvel of neatness, and offered metal chairs. Potts
sat behind his desk and began.

"I feel really funny about telling you this. Parker
LeMay seems like a nice enough guy, and he's always treated me good. When he asked me to go with
him to look at the crash, I went. Couldn't see why
not to. But…well, something happened a couple of
years ago and I kinda feel like he had something to
do with it."

The mechanic, obviously nervous, stopped to sip
from a cup of water. "I had a little sister. Lots
younger. Trisha. Well, Trisha, she went to work at
LeMay's company about three, four years ago. I
guess because of me. Parker was starting to be
around the airport a lot in those days and I met him.
I think he came out to fly right seat with some business acquaintance, give him a few tips. He'd flown
during Vietnam. Wouldn't fly himself, though, not
till he got together with you. Mentioned to him once

that my sister had just graduated and was looking for a job, and he said to send her around.

"Everything was fine for a while. She didn't mind the job. Met a fella. Things were going okay. Parker had her working on some special drugs and gave her a raise, she said. She was kinda proud about it. And then, well…I guess she just started to sort of fade. At first, I thought maybe she was pregnant. She was sick to her stomach a lot. And then the life just kinda went out of her. We all used to play a little touch football in the yard, fall afternoons. She used to love it. Ran like the devil. Really got into it. And then, like, suddenly she just watched on the sidelines." He stopped, remembering.

"I'll never forgive myself for not seeing how sick she really was. She had a couple of weeks vacation coming, and I suggested she go home, see the folks and take it easy. Let Mom take care of her. Parker told her to go and stay as long as she wanted. I thought then that he was being real sympathetic. Now I wonder if maybe he didn't want to get rid of her. Anyway, next thing I know, the phone rings and Dad tells me she died out there. She'd only just turned twenty. She hadn't been gone from here more than ten, twelve days. It was an awful shock to the folks."

I felt the chill in the office and shivered. "Oh, Jack, that's a terrible story. I'm so very sorry."

Potts swiped his eyes quickly with a shirtsleeve. "Thanks. It's okay now. I didn't mean to burden you two with my family trouble, but when I thought maybe you were going to get involved with LeMay again, I just needed to tell you about this.''

Albert, quietly listening until now, shifted on the hard metal chair. "Was there an autopsy done on her? And had she seen a doctor in your hometown? Had she seen anyone here?"

"She wouldn't go see anyone here. I think Parker sort of pooh-poohed it, made her feel like she was dogging it. Mom said they sent her to our old family doc, but he just said he thought it was some kind of bug, and she'd get over it. She was buried in our small town cemetery, next to her grandparents. They aren't much on autopsies out there. I don't think we'll ever know what really killed her."

Albert sank into the chair as best he could, stretching his legs straight out in front. He looked thoughtful. We could hear the fan from the electric heater in the room. Outside, through the open hangar door, a plane started taxiing northeast. "I know you think that my medical training can shed some light on this, but I really doubt that it can," he said. "Maybe if I'd been able to see her in time. And maybe not." He tried a different tack. "Any idea what sort of work she was doing? What product she was working with? I mean, do you think she caught something that killed her?"

Potts pushed back from the desk and stood, his bearing almost military. He was daring us to make light of his theory. "That's what I believe. And I think LeMay was trying to keep her from doctors and get her out of town before anyone knew what it was."

Was this the same man with whom we'd been sharing a plane?

Then why did my heart go out to him? Because his funeral tears were real? Okay, there are worse reasons to respect a man, but could someone with compassion and feelings completely write off the illness of a young woman like Trisha Potts? Maybe, if she was in a position to blow a business he'd worked endlessly to develop. What was it Beebee Ballard had said, that she thought LeMay's business had been on the ropes at one time? A worker catching some virulent bug in a lab, a bug that might be contaminating the lab's products, would have to be considered very bad news indeed.

Interesting, and of course, tragic, but Jack Potts's story had nothing, really, to do with the problems at hand. Still, the landscape was becoming littered with death.

TEN

"ANY IDEA WHAT Potts was doing Thursday night?" I asked Albert. "Nice man and all, but..." We were far enough past the hangar to be heard.

"I asked him. So had the cops, apparently. Home with his wife and her mother. Pot roast on Thursdays."

"Looks like there could be motive in that story somewhere."

"And what about that Westgaard business? Until the funeral, I didn't even know LeMay knew him. Sounded like trouble." Albert looked somber for a moment, but the airport always cheered him.

If we'd simply walked through the back door to our car, we would have missed the jet sitting on the apron not far from our hangar. Albert, however, wanted to walk the long way round just for the fun of checking out the planes, and there it was. There, that is, they were. Qualls, his men, a couple of pilots. Someone was loading the small amount of luggage into the back area of a sleek eight-seat Citation. The man with the problem arm was talking to a pilot. Qualls himself was standing alone.

"Mr. Qualls!" I said, more than pleased at this unexpected meeting.

He was high on the list of people I hoped to interview. I think I startled him, though. He shuddered slightly, peering over his shoulder at the sound of my voice. He'd shed the Brioni jacket for something casual but nice. The fancy rags covered him the way Dior's Poison would cover a bad case of body odor, which is to say, not completely. Something leaked out.

Albert was mildly startled, too. He'd been too busy looking at the plane to notice the people around it. I knew his admiration of the beautiful little jet had nothing to do with desire. He didn't covet corporate jets and neither did I, at least not until I had to drive to our commercial airport in a blizzard. Flying at thirty-five thousand feet was fine but anonymous. Hard to wave to a farmer in his field from thirty-five thousand feet. Hard to see irrigation systems at work, a train on its lonely track, the small towns of America going about their daily work, as we had always done in *Sweet Juliet*. My, my, was that me thinking such positive thoughts about small planes? My voice, in any case, jarred the two men loose. Interrupted from other thoughts, they recovered and came together, shaking hands the second time in two days.

"I guess we shouldn't be surprised to see you," I said. "You mentioned you were leaving soon, so obviously you'd be leaving from here."

"Not necessarily." Cold. Very cold.

"Nice plane," said Albert, jumping right in.

"Thanks." Qualls turned all the way toward him, leaving me contemplating his back. "We have a bigger jet back home, but the Citation is the one we prefer. I was about to ask if you flew from here.

Then I remembered. Guess you'll be renting for a while." He pulled a pipe from his pocket and began the arduous task of trying to fill and light it. A pipe? If it was the affectation I thought it was, I wondered what 1920s fiction he was using for guidance. Gatsby, maybe. "We rent from here sometimes," he said, pulling hard and fast at the stem. "Just fooling around when we're in town. Like the trainer, the Mustang, they have out here. Ever seen it?"

"The P-51? Yeah, I've seen it. Always wanted to try it. Spitfires pass through here sometimes, too."

"My pilot likes those things. I don't fly, of course, but I do go up with him when he takes the trainer. Longtime military plane nut."

Albert nodded. "Don't you fantasize air battles?"

"Sometimes." They were off on a World War II nostalgia trip, comparing the relative worth of fighters long gone.

All this plane talk was losing me. The breeze that was turning brisk carried a bit of real cold, making me shiver. We'd have our first snow soon, the usual October surprise.

This guy was about to return to Kansas City and I'd likely never see him again. Whatever he knew would fly away with him. I glanced at his plane again, depressed, and noticed beside it on the ground a box about the size of a computer case, with markings in red. I couldn't quite make out the symbol, but the word "Hazardous" leaped out.

"What's that?" I asked, interrupting a discussion of air battles over Britain.

Qualls looked where I was pointing. "The box?

Oh, that's nothing, a little cesium 137 we're taking back to work with.'' The pipe was finally lit. Albert had made him comfortable. He was actually willing to elaborate. ''There's some other radioactive material that's used medically in there, too. Strontium 90. P32. LeMay's stuff.'' He took a puff, allowing the fragrant smoke to billow out. ''Need to check the quality, since we're planning the merger.''

''Bacteria?''

''No, of course not. No bacteria. No viruses. No vegetable matter from alien star systems. Just tracers, mostly.'' He glanced at Albert. ''You have a very curious wife.''

''Heightened sensitivity since our plane crash,'' he said.

Qualls's face turned stony. ''Nothing here has anything to do with your plane crash. Your police even had the nerve to ask for *my* whereabouts the night before the crash.''

I was annoyed, which made me brazen. ''And where were you?''

''Not that it's any concern of yours, but I was in Kansas City, where I'd been all week with my men. And now, I'm sorry. I must leave.''

We muttered good-byes. Albert took my arm and moved me along, out of hearing and away from the newly shampooed Citation. He didn't say anything more until we'd edged between two adjacent buildings and found the street out back and started toward our car. Even then, he looked around before mentioning what was troubling him. ''Why are you bothering that guy? Something about him makes me very uncomfortable.'' He frowned. ''I wish you'd leave him alone. For that matter, him and this whole Parker LeMay business. It's enough, already.''

''Okay, fine. And I guess he has an alibi. Maybe. But what is he doing flying around with radioactive material in the plane? How would you like to be sharing space with a box like that?''

''I spend every day of my life sharing space with hot elements. Well, anyway,'' he amended, ''they're somewhere in my building. Tritium isotopes. Radioactive iodine for thyroid work. Cobalt 60 for cancer sometimes, and believe me, that's plenty hot. Remember the heart CAT scan your mother had last year? Doesn't work without radioactive thallium. Fact of medical life, that stuff. Has been since the war your friend and I were just talking about.''

''Three Mile Island. Chernobyl. Don't they scare you?''

''Sure they do. And I don't work with it much at all compared to some others.'' We found the car, now in late-afternoon shadows. Once the kind October sun sank low in the sky, the chill I'd noticed earlier increased, a definite warning of winter. Albert put the information on the new plane carefully in the glove compartment. ''Why don't you ask your sons about this if you're so interested? They know more than I do. I think they both had to do papers on the Manhattan Project last year. Something about history through the invention of weapons. I love the way they teach these days.''

And I did, though by the time we got home, said sons were totally decompressed. Paul was splayed before a Nickelodeon program, reliving his childhood. Spence had logged on to some game room. The half hour before dinner was the least productive time for all of us in any twenty-four-hour period. I informed the heirs that when the TV was over, I needed fifteen minutes of their valuable assistance. That gave me a needed quarter hour of my own to pour a pepper vodka for Albert, a ginless gin and tonic for me, and then to pace. My head was too full of the day to wind down completely. Besides, I wanted my boys to brainstorm with me. Albert was going through the mail, sneaking little peeks at the photo of the Turbo Arrow between bills. He was, for now, useless.

In due course, I had my sixteen-year-olds. I stole a minute to admire their beauty, my wonderful babies, and then made them sing for their supper. Moving us all to the game table in the corner of the great room, I informed them that I needed to know everything they knew about radioactivity.

"Oh, Mom, it's been a year since we studied that stuff!"

"That's okay. This isn't a test. I just want you to remember whatever you can."

"Like half-lifes and stuff?"

"Sure. Anything." I would have to check what they told me, but this wasn't a bad place to begin.

Paul, the numbers person, remembered the figures, as I knew he would. "Plutonium's really cool. Of course, it's also seriously expensive. Only about a million dollars a pound or so. Its half-life isn't for more than twenty-four thousand years. Uranium takes a long time, too. But that's bomb stuff. Are you planning a hit?''

"She's bombing the Educational Testing Service or whatever it's called," said Spence. "Before next week." The upcoming exams were obviously on his mind.

"Good move!" cheered Paul. "But after they're gone, don't forget you have to bury the waste products. No sticking it in our barrels on trash day. And you'll need something correct to put it in. Lead containers, maybe. Some TV show said Russia's been injecting the stuff directly underground without anything around it and it's starting to show up in rivers.''

"Not to mention illegal, at least in America," added Spence. "Junking hot waste is a big, expensive deal around here.''

"It sure is at the hospital," said Albert from across the room. "It costs six hundred a barrel here, and a barrel doesn't hold much. In the east, I hear, they're up to three thou.''

"How do you know that? I thought you didn't have much to do with that stuff.''

"Largely true," said Albert, stuffing the plane papers into a desk. "Now and then I deal with something hot.''

"Ever work with any of Parker's products?" I hated asking. "Tracers, maybe?''

"Who knows? I don't order the stuff.''

I turned back to the boys. "Is any of it safe?''

The boys looked at each other and shook their heads. "Uh-uh," said Paul. "Not if you get enough of it. Remember that story about Edison's technician? Mrs. Rayburn told it to us.''

"Oh, right.'' Spence obligingly picked up the ball. "In the early 1900s, Edison was trying to develop a fluoroscope. You know, just an ordinary fluoroscope. Grandma told us years ago, shoe stores had them. She used to love sticking her feet in there, wiggling her toes to see if the new shoes had enough room. She could see the bones. Anyway, this technician spent so much time working on the glass and everything that eventually he got what turned out to be radiation burns on his hands. And then he died. Of radiation sickness.''

"Heavens!''

"That taught him to suck up to the boss,'' added Spence.

Millie came into the room to announce that dinner was ready. Now. Millie's dinner waited for no man, woman, or child. We headed for the dining room, my mind racing down some of the myriad paths that lead to sleepless nights.

Dinner was a relatively quiet affair, each of us uncharacteristically self-absorbed. By the time Beebee called around nine, everyone had peeled off in different directions, leaving me the bedroom phone undisturbed.

"Well, I've turned up about all I can on your two companies,'' she announced. "That's not a party. That's my quiet, restrained family. Just us. Can't you tell?''

"Okay, lady, if you say so. I couldn't put together a laundry list with such a racket."

She laughed. "This is nothing! White noise. Let me tell you what I found, such as it is." She began with a string of numbers, mostly referring to Bio-Quest. Gross annual sales. Estimated net worth. Imports and exports. Out of context, none of it meant much to me. "They seem healthy enough. Of course, numbers lie. Qualls bought the controlling interest in this company only two years ago, and word is he's a smart-enough money man. Not that anyone I talked to really knows him. He seems to have emerged as a player nationally only about, maybe, six or eight years ago. My sources didn't agree on where he came from, what he did before, nothing. They all agreed that he made them nervous, however. Nobody seems to have been able to approach him."

She stopped to shout something at the noise behind her before continuing. "Qualls surrounds himself with a couple of henchmen who move in when anyone gets too close. Or so I hear. Anyway, so much on that end.

"Parker LeMay's company is more interesting, and easier to track. He started it, very undercapitalized, about fifteen years ago. And it was a struggle. There was even a Chapter Eleven on record, but he seems to have worked through that. Still, it showed minimal growth until about eighteen, twenty months ago. Then suddenly, the figures shoot up. As you know, eventually he took it public. Pretty impressive after such a rocky start. What turned it around? No one seems to know. His product mix stayed pretty much the same, but... Hey, I don't know. I'm just a money lady. You're the detective.''

"Hah.''

"Anything else I can do for you? I'm really into this now.'' She had to shout to be heard.

"Not for the moment. Thanks. I'll keep you posted, promise.''

I hung up, stretched out across the bed, and picked absently at the stitches that quilted the down comforter. Who had waved a magic wand at Parker, making all his troubles disappear? I needed to find that out. Turnarounds like that don't just happen.

Millie, I suddenly realized, must have noticed the chill today, too. She'd switched to the heavy quilt, our winter bedding. Albert's pajama bottoms, the only part he wore, were on his pillow, neatly folded. On my side, she'd put a thin flannel nightgown, another sign that she had decided the night would be cold. If Millie decides it will be cold, better light a fire. She controls the weather. Even though it was early, I stripped off my jeans and sweater and slipped into the soft nightie. Albert believes there's nothing in the world more seductive than a woman wrapped head to toe in Laura Ashley flannel. That's okay with me. I like the feel of flannel against my skin, too.

Since Albert wouldn't be coming to bed, and to my flannel, anytime soon, I burrowed into the down pillows to think. Beebee's information didn't mean anything obvious, but it was promising. I wondered what had happened to make the LeMays rich. Or anyway, his company successful. I really didn't know if they were rich, actually. Tomorrow, without fail, I would start to interview some of the people I needed to see. And the one I was going to start with was LaShawn, Parker and Jann's housekeeper. I'd have to wait to call over there till I was pretty sure Parker had gone to work. If he answered, I'd hang up. What if he had that Call Whatever that displayed the names of people who had dialed their number? What if Wednesday was the help's day off? What if she'd already quit? What if she wouldn't talk to me? What if I died before morning?

ELEVEN

APPARENTLY, THE AMATEUR detective is blessed with luck, probably to make up for the fact that she's flying blind. At my first try the next morning, LaShawn answered the phone. I told her that I was working on a story about the Vietnamese in America who had made good and asked if she'd be willing to talk to me about Jann. She agreed, somewhat reluctantly, if I didn't take too long. I mentioned that Parker probably shouldn't be told about the interview so soon after his wife's tragic death. If she found that curious, she didn't say. Consequently, eleven o'clock found me in the foyer of the loft, unusually quiet at this time of day with none of the bustle one would assume in a multi-unit downtown property. I rang an appropriate buzzer, choosing from the collection set into a brushed steel panel. LaShawn answered, led me in, and seated me at a chrome-and-glass kitchen table. The place smelled of Windex and disinfectant. No music came from the small radio on the counter but I suspected, before I rang, it had.

She had recovered her composure. The grief I'd seen after the memorial service was gone. If anything, it had been replaced with distrust. There was no offer of coffee or anything else. She eyed my tape recorder and steno notebook warily.

She looked great in black Lycra stretch pants and a heather tunic. The clothes were more comfortable than she was, however. Her body language was pure attitude. "You're not really writing an article, are you." It wasn't a question and I didn't respond. "You're just prying, trying to figure out what happened here. For some reason."

I rubbed one of my loafers against the leg of my jeans. I felt like I'd been caught by the teacher with gum. "Yeah, okay, I'm not doing the article I told you I was," I admitted. "The accident that killed Jann could easily have killed us. And, of course, it was no accident. I don't know if Parker told you, but we shared the plane with him. I need to find out what really happened, and I think you could help."

Her look softened slightly. She seemed to decide I was okay. I could feel her reluctance erode. She played with flawlessly manicured nails, nails that denied the housework she did for a living. The braids were as precise as an algebraic equation. "I loved Jann," she said. "No one in my life has ever been as nice to me, as caring as she was. Everyone thought she was cold but she wasn't. Anyway, not to me. So if I can help you or anyone else find out who made her die in such a terrible way, you bet I'll help."

"Thanks." I automatically took out my notebook. "How long have you worked here?"

"Six years, almost. Parker was wrong the other day."

"Full time?"

"Just mornings. Afternoons, I go to class at the

extension. Down the street. Trying to get a B.A. in history."

"Getting close?"

"Two years, about, till I'm finished." She turned shy. "I'd really like to work in government someday. Jann said I could do it and that she'd help when the time came. She said she'd talk to the governor."

She hoped that, even with Jann gone, the governor would remember her when the time came. She'd met him a number of times, made lunch for the two of them now and then when they needed to escape from the busy office to get some quiet work done. But even if he didn't remember, or if Merriwell wasn't in office anymore by the time the degree came through, she'd make it somehow. Jann had taught her what persistence would do. And yes, she was going to continue to work here. She needed the money, and besides, the loft was close to her school. And Parker?

"He's okay, I guess. Kind of creepy. I think he was a little jealous of the relationship Jann and I had. He'd try to be friendly to me, but I just couldn't stand his getting near me, not physically and not in any other way. Not that he tried anything, I don't mean that. He was very devoted to Jann. But he just sort of turned me off. Fortunately, it looks like I won't be seeing much of him. He's usually gone by the time I get here in the morning and, as I told you, I only put in half a day. Clean up the place. Make him a little dinner and put it in the fridge. He leaves my pay for me, plus grocery money. At least, that's what he's done the last couple of days. We're still working things out. After all, it's only been since Friday that Jann is gone.''

"Do you think there was any possibility that Jann was involved with anyone else? Or that Parker was?'' My memory, unbidden, played back Hallie's answering machine.

"Oh no, not a chance. I mean, I can't imagine such a thing. Those two were so totally *married*. But…''

"But?''

"Well, I did use to wonder about the governor sometimes. It was like he couldn't leave her alone. Was after her all the time. He used to call when Jann was home for some reason. If she had a cold, for instance. I'd know because I answered the phone, usually. Then, when she was still on the phone with him, if I came into the room, she'd get real quiet. And she'd wait till I was gone before she started talking again.'' She rose gracefully to her feet. "Say, want a Coke or something? I would.''

I wasn't about to reject an offer of any kind, not when this lady was being so helpful. She opened two cans from the fridge and handed me one, making no move to find a glass. I took a swallow, tasting the aluminum. "You were talking about the governor.''

"Yeah.'' She drank, her nails clicking against the can. "There was one time he came over here to talk. They were in the office back there.'' She gestured with her head. "I was bringing them some coffee when the phone rang. I heard her tell the caller that she didn't know where the governor was, but she thought he'd gone to the western slope on vacation for at least three days. I mean, she lied for him, and probably more than once.''

"Then why are you so sure there was nothing going on between them? It certainly sounds like they were hiding *something*.''

She sighed, shaking her head. "It wasn't there. Any electricity. A gal like me knows these things. But yeah, they did seem to be hiding something, at least from me. Jann got real tense sometimes after she'd been with him. But honestly, I don't think they were, you know, involved.''

I decided to try a different tack. "Does the name Hallie mean anything to you?''

"Oh, I don't know. Maybe I've heard it." A surprising Mickey Mouse clock ticked loudly on the wall. She glanced at it.

"Ever hear Parker use it? Could she have been a friend of his?'' I remembered how quickly, and subversively, he'd rescued that phone number from Jann's purse.

"I don't know. Maybe once or twice. I think I heard him use that name. Or maybe it was Mailin. Say, do you have a lot more? My class starts at one and I still have a few things to do here.''

I moved to the edge of my chair. "Sorry. I'll hurry. Just a couple of things. What about her sister, now that you mentioned her. What was that argument about the other day?''

"Mailin? She and Jann fought sometimes. And she fought with Parker, too. She lived here. Did you know that? She moved out the day after Jann died.

Saturday." She shook her head with disgust. "A freeloadin' woman. Completely. She had a few jobs after she came over a couple of years ago, but none of them lasted. She'd hang here, getting in my way. She liked to order me around. Watched a lot of TV. She was cheap. Dressed flashy. Looked like trouble, and I wouldn't be all that surprised if she was. She had money from somewhere. I didn't like her."

I had a feeling that if LaShawn didn't like a person, that person was likely to notice.

"Any idea what they fought about?"

She laughed. "Are you kidding? No way could I understand them. Mailin was taking that English as a Second Language but when they fought, they fought in their *first* language. And I'll bet it was plenty ugly. It upset Jann a lot. Mailin was the one person who could make Jann cry."

I thought of the Jann I remembered, tall, gorgeous, expensively groomed, and always poised. "Hard to imagine her in tears. Out of control." I took a chance. "Any possibility I might have a look at Mailin's room?"

"I haven't had a chance to clean it up yet," she said, standing to lead the way. "You'll be able to tell what a total slob she was." We started together toward the back of the loft while the housekeeper-slash-student continued. "Once Jann wouldn't have cried, you know, but she changed a lot over the last few months. I don't know if it was Mailin's fault or not, but she wasn't herself. She sort of, I don't know... She sat around more, didn't bustle here and there moving furniture and filling vases with flowers she'd buy. Like she used to. I think it was Mailin really stressin' her out.'' She picked up the pace of her walk. ''My ma used to say, you can't choose your relatives.''

The room was large and high-ceilinged. I wondered if that space had existed as a room before the arrival of the little sister. Lofts are usually vast and undefined. Jann must have cared enough for the comfort of her sister to have someone build an enclosing wall.

The bedding had been pulled off and thrown in the corner of the room and one end of the exposed mattress lay half off the springs. A dusting of what looked like face powder covered the top of a contemporary highboy near the closet. The drawers seemed to have been emptied and then left at varying states of closure. A small desk under one huge industrial window sported three very distinct cigarette burns. Posters seemed to have been stuck to the walls with tape and then ripped off, leaving jagged corners. The room smelled odd, old perfume and something else. The place was airless.

LaShawn must have smelled it, too. She wrestled with the huge window, finally lifting it a crack. ''Nice, huh? I guess I better get to work in here before Parker gets home tonight and finds it still looking like this.''

I moved to the other side of the window to see if I could help her open it a bit wider. Something flashed behind the desk. As LaShawn watched, I moved the small piece of furniture away from the wall, reached down, and snared the glittery object.

It was a ring, a small one, the size a child would wear. We looked at it together, silently. On the flat face of the gold circle crest was a character in what looked like Chinese. Nothing was inscribed inside. There wouldn't have been room on such a little band to write, but a cunning spiral design etched the lifted side of the face. It looked like eighteen-karat gold, a beautifully made small symbol of a jeweler's art.

"Oh, you found this. You snooping, you couldn't wait." The voice was loud and angry and LaShawn and I both jumped. "I knew I did not find it in my stuff."

Mailin Duong was in the doorway, glaring at us both but mostly me. She'd cut her hair short since the funeral and it capped her head tightly. The "do" implied control. She didn't have it, not even close. The voice was shrill. "Who are you? You want to buy ring? Or just to steal it."

"Hello, Mailin," I said as coolly as possible. "My name is Grace Beckmann. I knew your sister." I held out the ring. "Is this yours? It was behind the desk. You must have dropped it, or maybe Jann did."

"That's mine." She grabbed it and stuffed it loosely into the coin purse of her wallet. With the two of us staring back at her, she seemed for the moment uncertain. Her voice, however, was hardly less confrontational. "I need to look again in here. Maybe left other things."

LaShawn nodded. "Mmm-hmmm. I've got work to do." She turned to me, making a face Mailin couldn't see. "Nice meeting you. Call me if you think of anything else." And she was gone.

Mailin watched her leave and then, with arms folded across her chest, waited for me to explain myself. I straightened.

"I'm a writer. And, as I said, we, my husband and I, knew your sister." For maybe the millionth time in my life, I wished I were a more accomplished liar. "My editor at the magazine is interested in a piece about the Vietnamese experience in America. Would you be willing to let me interview you? After you're through going through your room, of course."

"What magazine?"

Oops. *"Smithsonian."* If she checked, I was in trouble big time. Maybe I should just have said I was at the query stage.

"Well…" She pondered for a long moment. With the harsh light of late morning painting her face, she looked haggard. My original estimate of someone in the mid to late thirties still held. Her hands were young, her neck barely lined; she couldn't have been too much older. But the face. It looked like it had endured decades, not years, of trouble. I was almost sorry my cover story about an article was a phony. Maybe when all this business about *Sweet Juliet* was over, I really could turn some of my interviews into a sale.

She fooled with the cuffs of a smart linen blouse. Her clothes looked nothing at all like the cheap, too-short outfit she'd had on at the memorial service. These clothes, I'd bet, were from her sister's closet.

She spoke, her tone ironic. "My experience in America, I don't think your editor would like. Would print. Jann's, maybe."

"Jann's would be fine. You probably knew her better than anyone. Or at least, anyone but Parker. Tell me your story and hers, too."

She hesitated a long minute. "Yes. Okay. I guess. But not now."

We made a date to meet the next day, late morning, in the lobby of the city's grandest old hotel, a landmark of grace and gentility. I figured the ambience would be calming and at the same time anonymous. Newspaper types often interviewed their subjects in a corner of the oversized couches, where even celebrities are ignored by those coming and going. If Mailin decided to trust me, we could segue into lunch in the pleasant dining room. That would give me an extra hour with her.

Leaving the loft finally after strained good-byes, I retrieved my car from a nearby lot. I pulled the Aurora into lower downtown traffic, mulling the morning. LaShawn was more helpful than she knew. Did the governor visit Jann at her loft when LaShawn was gone for the day and off at her classes? Obviously, Jann lied for him, but that was probably par for the course in politics. An affair? Maybe. How much did Parker know about those visits? And Mailin, with that ring. So angry over a baby ring. She'd have to tell me tomorrow. I wouldn't let her off the hook till I knew that story.

But now, I had to switch gears into my more pedestrian life. Albert's string quartet was meeting at our house tonight, which meant I had to provide some kind of munchies. Probably something sweet, since they were working on the Mozart A Major Quintet and wouldn't finish till after the ten o'clock news. The quartet had played together for years and knew how to work as a team. Tonight, though, they were importing a clarinetist, so all bets were off. If I were a really good person, I'd stay up and wrestle with the espresso machine. Give them a serious caffeine jolt to get them home safely. If I were an even better person than that, I'd ask Millie to bake, but that good a person I wasn't. I'd driven about a block and was debating about which bakery to head for when I felt the bang against my rear bumper. More than a bang, really. More like a real crash. My head flew forward, then back. I heard the crunch of breaking glass and thought of the car's mega-size rear lights. Oh, rats, rats, rats. I loved this car. How could some troglodyte plow into me when I wasn't even stopped?

I jammed on the brakes and checked the rearview mirror, intending to glare at the culprit. A large, dark American sedan was backing up and swinging around to the left. I caught a glimpse of someone through smoked glass, a man, turning deliberately away from me as he passed my window. A tennis-type white hat with all-around floppy brim hid his face completely. Since, even at such a quick glance, I could tell he wasn't wearing tennis clothes, something seemed way off the mark, but he was gone before I could register much else.

I pulled to the side of the downtown street and

got out to examine the damage. My heart sank when I saw the car's backside.

"He did that deliberate, lady." One of the vestiges of the area's erstwhile wino population shuffled past me, pointed, and nodded knowingly. The wind blew his filthy maroon parka up across a deep tear. He stopped for a minute, maybe remembering a time when he might have been able to offer some help. Then he shrugged apologetically and moved on. I knelt down to examine the crunched chrome, checking to make sure I could drive the car without having a sharp end dig into my tires. I had maybe an inch to spare, but at least I could get home without incurring any more damage. It occurred to me that I should probably call the police and report the crash-and-run, but forget it. I'd let our insurance guy deal with this. I just wanted to get out of this neighborhood.

I straightened up and, as I did, I thought I caught sight of the tennis hat speeding away from my car and down the block. The man, whoever he was, ran hard for fifteen yards or so and then slowed to a jog, turning down an alley that he seemed to know was there. He had been near my open window while I was down groveling around the tire. I was afraid to look inside the car.

Nothing horrible had been left on the seat. A note was there, but it might have been something really awful. I was afraid of…well, never mind what I was afraid of. Sometimes it's hazardous to drive a pretty car in a dicey area. And red cars don't meld into the background. Vandalism wasn't exactly unknown anywhere in the city, and certainly not in these newly gentrified blocks.

On the beige leather upholstery was a message scrawled on a piece of lined notebook paper, like that in a high school notebook. I got into the driver's seat, closed the window, locked the doors, and picked it up. My hands were shaking, just a little, but enough so reading was turning into a real trick. The note, in printed Magic Marker, was short but perfectly clear. "Get lost."

Well, it could have been worse. One would think that anyone going to such lengths to deliver a message would make the message itself a little more terrifying. My car would be out of commission for at least a week so I knew whoever it was meant business, but still, the whole experience lacked ferocity. I crumpled the note in my fist and turned on the engine. It started, purring as though no one in the world wished it ill.

Albert needn't know about this. I'd tell him a car hit me at a stoplight. In the meantime, I was making someone nervous and that was okay. Maybe.

TWELVE

THE ONLY WAY I could get through the evening was to repress the note and the "accident" totally. I greeted all the regular members of the quartet, met the clarinetist who was new to the group, offered goodies, coffee, soft drinks, ice, and retired upstairs. I could still hear them, but faintly. Fortunately, I'd been able to find some leftover pecan tarts and brownies in the freezer. Didn't quite make it to the bakery.

By the next day, unseasonable warmth had returned, reaffirming October as the year's most beautiful month. Albert had decided that, sabbatical or no, he wasn't getting anything done at home. Too many distractions. He'd started going back to the hospital library in the mornings as if he were still hurrying to early rounds. I'd hoped he'd be in enough of a rush to miss the damage, but no such luck. Seconds after he hit the garage, he was back.

"What in the world happened to your car?"

I drained the last of my Dark Italian Roast and tried to look sheepish. "A little accident."

"Did you back into something?"

"Actually, something forwarded into me." If he hadn't noticed the crumpled rear, I would have been perfectly capable of keeping quiet, but I can't lie outright, and certainly not to Albert. No one has ever recommended total exposure as a requisite of good marriages. Don't ask, don't tell works on the domestic front, too, but lying is different. It's always been my theory that liars are created when the truth is punished too harshly. Those lied to are, in a way, more at fault that those doing the lying. The whole scene is demeaning to both parties. Or maybe I just espouse all these theories because I'm such a lousy liar.

So Albert heard the story. All of it. He disappeared for a minute toward the kitchen and when he returned, he had his own coffee and the portable phone.

"All right, we're going to call Detective Morrisey and tell him all about this. It's a very serious matter, this threat."

"Oh, now let's lose all the melodrama. The note was hardly that scary." Unfortunately, I no longer totally believed what I was saying. My strange elation at provoking a response had, during the night, segued into something a little like fear. I knew I was worried when I didn't mention the "accident" to my mother during the seven-fifteen phone call. Besides, she was having her own problems.

"I'm really worried about this dreadful woman who moved into the next unit."

"Why? Is she sick?"

"No, no. Quite the contrary. Hale and hearty. Wants to go all the time. Every museum trip. Every card game. Every group that decides to inflict their music-making on us. Everything."

"So?"

"She wants me to go with her."

I laughed. "So you hooked a live one for a neighbor. Could be worse."

"No, it most certainly could not. I have my routines. I have my soap operas. Tell me how to handle this."

So this was my problem, but what else was new? "Okay, I'll think about it. Here, Millie wants to say hi." I handed over the phone, knowing it was safe. Millie hadn't seen the car yet so she couldn't blow the whistle.

That, however, was an hour ago. The fear was abating, but hadn't left. Albert reached over and closed the paper I was pretending to read. "I have something else to tell you. I was going to wait till later, but that was before I saw your car." He looked more serious than usual.

"Well?"

"Last night. You know, we were playing with a clarinet. We ended up having to wait a lot for him. He's not used to us. Normally, I have to concentrate but last night I had too much time to think. I remembered hearing this quintet at a chamber music concert last spring with Jeff, our violist. He works with P32. Radioactive phosphorus. Maybe that was the connection that triggered this." He tried the coffee, still too hot to drink. "Anyway, whatever the reason, my mind wandered and suddenly I remembered that container they found in *Sweet Juliet*. I realized what it must have been. And then I just knew what was almost certainly wrong with Trisha Potts, Jack's sister. It's the one thing that makes the most sense." His concentration drifted and he stopped.

Certainly after sixteen years of marriage I knew when to keep quiet, but it was all I could do.

Finally, he emerged from his distant regions. "It was a pig."

"Excuse me?"

"A pig. A container used to store radioactive material. I've never seen one quite like that, but I think that's what it must have been."

"But there wasn't anything in it."

"I know. And that's very curious, because Jann took it with her in the plane and crashed only a few minutes later. I suppose she might have thrown the contents out the window, but somehow I have the feeling she was too busy trying to survive to fiddle with that."

"It was wrapped up. Maybe she didn't know it was empty."

"Maybe. Not inconceivable. Maybe she thought there was something hot in it. After all, we know Parker makes radioactive tracers. He must create a lot of waste like the boys were telling you about. You're not supposed to get rid of it yourself. It's the government's job. In theory. I heard somewhere that the Mafia has been involved with dumping it."

"You're kidding!" I couldn't believe that. "Can't you just imagine some mob guy running around with a bag of lab trash?"

"The whole thing is ridiculous." He glanced at his watch. I suspected he wanted to wait to call the police till Morrisey got in. "I talked to Jeff after the session last night. Poor guy, he probably thought I'd never let him go home. Asked him a lot of questions. The idea that someone would throw hot waste out of an airplane window struck him as ludicrous. But he did confirm that disposal's a problem.'' He brushed toast crumbs from his lap.

"I'm beginning to get the message. You're suggesting that Trisha had radiation sickness. What the boys were talking about yesterday.'' I frowned, trying to put it together. Jack Potts had said...well, what? Just that his sister had no energy, or had I missed something? "Suggestive, but not really convincing. I'd need more than that to blow any whistles.''

"Obviously, there's no longer any way to be sure, but if she hadn't been protected from something radioactive, certain types of symptoms would be likely, depending on the dose and how long she was exposed.''

"Like what?''

"Well, nausea for sure. Vomiting, diarrhea, infection.''

"Hey, I had all of those last winter. The kids brought the flu home from school.''

"And people used to die of the flu, remember?''

"Yeah, well...'' I sat back, dubious. "That's not what we're talking about.''

"No, we're talking about rads. The dose of radiation absorbed by the body. Jeff brought me up to speed on this last night. Five thousand rads and the central nervous system collapses. Everyone's dead in twenty-four hours. Six hundred or so and everyone still dies but it takes a couple of weeks. Hits the GI tract. A dose around half that and some people can survive, depending on all sorts of factors. Even the ones who do die can take as long as six weeks to do it. The radiation goes to the bone marrow, so people tend to die of infection. That sounds like what may have happened to Trisha."

I found myself shivering. "That's horrible, a young girl just starting out in life. Parker should be shot if he allowed that to happen."

"Let's call Morrisey." Albert produced the card the detectives had left and dialed the circled number. He was only, maybe, three feet away, but I honestly didn't hear what he was saying. Images kept appearing. The container, the "pig," from the plane. The box marked "Hazardous." Jann LeMay herself chose that moment to walk through my mind, ambitious, poised, elegant. She couldn't have been involved with this, no matter what she had with her when she died. She didn't work at Parker's lab, and she was much too busy with the governor to spend much time hanging around there. Certainly, no one could question the cause of her death. Only the why of it. And the who.

I moved out of my altered brain state in time to hear Albert click off with Detective Morrisey. He pushed down the phone's antenna and made the necessary moves to get up and go to work. "Morrisey is concerned about that car incident. He wants you to be very careful. Someone is obviously aware that you're snooping around. I also told him my theory that the container was a pig."

"Did he listen?"

"He already knew. Someone in his department had recognized it. It's time to stop playing detective here. Leave it to the pros. Things are getting too dangerous. Seriously."

I decided this wasn't the time to tell him about my appointment with Mailin later in the morning. Fortunately, Paul and Spence arrived at the breakfast table and created their usual major diversion. Albert, at last, made it out the door. Paul plunked about a hundred books on the table and poured himself some juice. Spence was carrying a handheld computerized blackjack game and nothing else. I looked at it and shook my head.

"You're not taking that to school."

Spence seemed genuinely startled. "Why not? I need something to do while everyone else crams for these dumb tests. The teachers don't stay in the room."

"Oh, for heaven's sake, Spence!" The PSATs were Saturday, two days away. It was probably too late to worry about the outcome anyway. Every kid in the class would be studying and my Spence would be playing blackjack. He'd end up with scores in the 300s, I figured. Paul, at least, might get into a good school. No one said that twins had to go to college together. Of course, there could be problems on Parents' Weekend. Whatever, I was too full of other thoughts to struggle effectively. I tried for a few objections, found them all effectively countered, and gave up. Spence kept the game.

They were out the door, leaving a vacuum behind

them, when Millie walked in to clear the table. Distracted, I didn't look up till I heard her clear her throat meaningfully. "Just wanted you to know I didn't tell your mother about the accident," she said. "But I did tell you when you bought that red car that red was pure trouble, so now you know." She exited self-righteously, stage left. Did I really think I could get anything past that woman?

By the time I headed for the downtown hotel, my poor, much-maligned car was in the body shop and I had acquired an inadequate rental. Something small and tinny. Now, I had even more questions Mailin had to answer for me whether she liked it or not. I just hoped her English was good enough for me to understand.

The hotel lobby was relatively quiet. A small queue was waiting to check out by the eleven-o'clock deadline, but a selection of dark red paisley couches was available, all with additional chairs and tables. I'd interviewed more than a few people here over the years and felt very much in my element. I spotted Mailin by the gold drinking fountain. She was wearing a gray pinstriped suit with belted jacket, almost certainly another of Jann's outfits, and one that was perfect for the time and place. Even so, she seemed uncomfortable, shifting from foot to foot and looking around. I began to regret not choosing a less intimidating venue.

I collected her, chose a spot away from other furniture clusters, and ordered tea for us both. Generally, it was all I could do to swallow tea, my idea of a dowager's drink, but I'd had enough coffee.

When Mailin ordered tea, it seemed politic to follow suit. I needed to keep her here, keep her happy, and keep her talking. We started with the basic questions: name, age, family in the States and in Vietnam.

She was thirty-six. Widowed. No children. Her mother (and Jann's) was still living in Ho Chi Minh City with her other child and lots of grandchildren. Things were okay there, but after Mailin's husband died working in the mountains, she became restless. She and Jann had always kept up with each other, writing letters every few months, so Mailin decided the time had come to see America herself. Certainly her sister had done well here, so maybe she could find a job or something for her. Jann sent her the money for the trip and she had arrived almost two years ago. That, at least, was her story.

And had things worked out for her?

Mailin took a sip of the steaming tea that had been brought in one of the hotel's fine flowered porcelain cups. Her eyes were dark. "It was terrible here. Jann give me the room you saw, but she never home. I was lonely. The jobs she found for me were bad jobs. Not good money. She said when I learn English it be better, but how I to learn when nobody home? Parker never like me. So I move out when Jann die."

"I noticed that you and Parker were having words the day of the memorial service."

"Yes. Someone tell police." She glanced at me, her eyes narrowing. "They ask where I was night before plane goes down. Like they think I..."

"Mmm," I said. Then dared, "And where were you?"

"I tell you, too, then. That none of their business. Or yours."

I waited till she calmed down a bit before back-pedaling. "Was Parker unhappy that you were leaving?"

"Hah. He very happy I leave. We fight because of Jann."

"What about Jann?"

She didn't object to the question. Just didn't answer it.

"Can I ask you about the ring I found? The baby ring?"

She shrugged and turned away. "Just that. Just a ring for a baby I knew." Again, I waited and hoped for more. And this time got it. "The baby died."

"Oh, how sad. Can you tell me what happened?"

"No." That was that.

I didn't bring a tape recorder for fear of spooking my "interview," but I did have my notebook. Thus far I'd been too gripped by the story to write down a word but the time had come. I didn't want her to go missing on me. "So where are you living now?"

She gave me the name of one of the city's more elegant residential hotels. "I stay there for a while. Maybe go back home soon. Now that Jann gone."

It was intrusive, but I had to ask. Journalists seem to be allowed obnoxious questions these days. "Mailin, forgive me for being so personal, but isn't that place awfully expensive? Since you don't have a job, I mean."

She smoothed a nonexistent wrinkle in one stocking. The sole of her shoe looked totally unworn. Could those have been Jann's, too, or had she bought them? "It doesn't matter, the money. I have it."

"Oh, of course. Jann must have left you something in her will."

She looked vague. "Will? Oh, maybe. It too soon."

I couldn't completely hide the fact that I was confused. Where was the money coming from? The outfit she was wearing at the memorial service had made her look like a lady of the evening, but her present dress of business suit and mid-high heels would hardly get it if she was depending for her rent money on a little illicit action. What, I wondered, was in that bag? Jann had carried a Louis Vuitton, or at least had the day she died. It was found in the plane. Mailin's purse was smaller but chic, probably a Chanel, and I had a very real urge to see her wallet. I wondered if she was the kind of person who would ring up big tabs in hotels and restaurants, and maybe department stores, and then skip out. People like that usually had very little cash. When my chance came to find out, I took it.

The flowers on all the tables were lavish and beautiful and probably fresh this morning. Consequently, they were making us both sneeze. When Mailin opened her purse to find a tissue, I pretended to reach across for something and lose my balance. A quick flick of my elbow and the purse was off the couch and splayed open on the floor. I bent over to help right the mess, and of course to check the wallet, but then immediately straightened back up. Scattered across the Oriental rugs, and blending in so thoroughly they were hard to see, were jewels. The contents of Mailin's purse looked like Tiffany's window after a hurricane. Antique gold bracelets mixed with earrings of precious and semiprecious stones. A huge tourmaline surrounded by diamonds had been made into a ring that would have turned heads at a Hollywood premiere. Two long strands of incredible pearls had a luster impossible to find at a costume jewelry counter no matter how long one might look. For a full minute, neither of us said a word.

Finally, I broke the startled silence. "Oh, Mailin, I'm so sorry. I must have slipped. Can I help you pick this up?"

"No." She bent over and swiftly collected the baubles, stashing them back into the small gray leather pouch. Then she stood angrily. "I am going."

I stood as well, talking fast to hide my discomfort. "Yes, well...I'm sorry we didn't have a chance to talk about Jann at all. Maybe some other time. But I have to tell you, you really shouldn't be carrying so much valuable jewelry in your purse. Anyone could steal it easily. Those pieces belong in a safe-deposit box, or at least in a safe place at home."

"They're fake." I couldn't tell, from the way the words spat out, if she was embarrassed or just furious. Whichever, I knew I wasn't going to get another crack at her if she could help it. And as for those rocks being paste, forget it. I'd seen my mother-in-law's collection. I knew what real looked like. Mailin wasn't about to hang around long enough to debate the issue, however. She pulled herself together, repacked the purse, and was ready to leave before I could catch my breath. Her exit speed from the hotel was just short of a run. Now what on earth was she doing with a small fortune in jewelry? Costly new shoes? New digs at one of the most expensive addresses in town?

I wasn't sure what to do next. Obviously, my chance at a nice lunch had just been lost. I'd even dressed up for the occasion. In skirt, T-neck, and blazer straight from the cleaner bag, heck, I looked pure Brooks Brothers. Or at least Lands' End. Even so, I'd scared off my quarry, and I hadn't even been able to ask if either LeMay had talked about the death of a young woman who had worked in the business. As it happened, I wondered if any question I might still have asked would have been as enlightening as that purse full of gold. For a woman with no visible means of support, she was certainly operating like a person of property. I wanted to debrief to Albert.

I wasn't sure what was happening to his office during his sabbatical so, rather than try the usual exchange, I rang his pager, leaving the number of one of the hotel's pay phones, and then stood there to guard it. People were beginning to drift toward the hotel grill which happened to be near the phone bank, laughing or talking intently to their companions. Music drifted in wisps from the nearby bar.

Working downtown, being part of that life, had always seemed very appealing. I'd married too young to be that focused and free.

In a minute or so, the phone rang. I told Albert about the events of the morning, bracing myself for the expected lecture. Amazingly, it didn't come.

"I did a little something re the 'problem' myself this morning, believe it or not. I talked to Parker."

"Wow, what struck you?"

"Well, you know what struck me. I asked him if Trisha Potts had been exposed to radiation."

"Whoa. How did he react?"

"Shocked at the question. There was a lot of dead air before he finally answered me. Then he said that the idea was ridiculous, that while some of his products were radioactive, he was always extremely careful with his workers. I think he was rattled. Even so, he agreed to meet me for a drink. There really was no way he could say no, since I let him choose the day."

And here I thought marriage held no more surprises. "That's great. Gutsy."

I could imagine him fiddling with a pencil, sensing my unasked question. "Radiation sickness is so devastating. It's a bad way to die." His voice turned authoritative. "Of course, we'll never be able to prove the Potts girl had it, but maybe Parker will break down when we get together."

We talked a bit more while I relished the idea that he was finally zoning in with me. People around me were dialing, talking, hanging up, but I didn't relinquish the phone. I was actually enjoying myself when the clinker came. He asked me if I'd go flying with him the next morning. He'd have to rent a plane, but that was no problem. He was used to my going along, conveniently ignoring the fact that I was doing it for him. No good deed goes unpunished. I was trying to find a reason to say no when he said he'd make a point of flying over the site where *Sweet Juliet* had gone down. He wanted to watch the distance measures, and then compare them with other times Jann or Parker had taken the plane. That would be fairly simple. There were logs.

That was different. How could I refuse?

THIRTEEN

I HUNG UP and pondered my options. The main branch of the library was just a few blocks away and, better yet, there was usually a cart selling hot dogs right outside. In my mind, that would compare favorably with lunch at the hotel, providing it came with gritty German mustard. I wanted to look up all sorts of things anyway. Maybe I could even check out a PSAT study book and make a last-ditch attempt to keep Spence from flunking. I wanted to read up on radiation. I needed to know more about the pharmaceutical business. Beebee had just whet my appetite. Most of this could be accessed by modem from our home computer, but for those of us who grew up around the musty-sweet smell of libraries, the only research that could be trusted was the kind we did at the source. We needed to touch the books, fondle the paper. A man in a green fishing jacket seemed to be waiting for my phone, so I moved away, sat on a tufted settee, and repacked my purse, putting the library card on top.

Someone should invent a dress purse that converts, with the switch of a few straps, to a fanny pack. Dress purses and libraries, I found, didn't mix. I was upstairs on the fourth floor in the business section juggling books, slips of paper, journals, my clutch purse, and a gaggle of pens. The hot dog was sitting uncertainly in my stomach. I had just dumped the whole armload of research possibilities on a large table when I heard the irrepressibly cheerful voice of my tardy tennis chum. I'd forgotten. Magda was a docent, and Thursday was her day.

"Hey, just the girl I wanted to see!"

"Hi. How's the docent business?"

"Quiet. But that's okay. I have plenty to do. I wanted to call you last night but it was too late by the time we got home."

I'd found three large books, eight journals, and a stack of loose Xeroxes so far. Magda moved them all to one side of the table and dropped into a sculpted wooden chair. She was wearing tights, walking shorts, and a loose blue cotton sweater, plain except for the official library badge pinned to it. From the back, she could have been eighteen. Apparently being on duty was no deterrent to sitting down with the customers. "Heard some inside dirt last night at this charity thing we had to go to and could hardly wait to tell you. About the gov. He really is supposed to be involved with someone. People have seen them. Apparently, he's really gaga over this one. It's more serious than most."

"Well, I guess that lets Jann out. She's not really much of a threat anymore, having been cremated."

"Oh, Grace, that's sick. And no, it doesn't let her out. The news isn't exactly up to date. Jann's been dead less than a week. It could still have been her." When things are too macabre, they begin sounding funny. We couldn't help it. We started laughing. Still, I didn't want to discourage Magda or anyone else from giving me the gossip. When you're collecting information, you don't send away the vendors.

"Well, a hot romance might explain a lot," I admitted. "The LeMay housekeeper reports lots of hush-hush phone calls and a few lies shared by Jann and the gov. Parker may have known about it. He sure was anxious to retrieve a certain phone number. It could—" I stopped suddenly.

Magda frowned. "What's wrong?"

"That man."

"What man?"

"In the green jacket. He just walked down that stack. He was at the hotel when I was, about an hour ago."

"So?"

I didn't want to go into the car accident with Magda. Without telling her about that, though, she wouldn't be able to understand why I felt crawly under my clothes. Was I being followed? I muttered something about needing to get on with my project but that I really appreciated her interest. She took the brush-off cheerfully, tucking an errant strand of my hair behind one ear, and disappeared toward the checkout desk.

As soon as she was out of sight, I grabbed my purse, leaving my books on the table, and ran down the few steps and left toward the stacks where I'd seen the man head in. His general body type, I suddenly realized, was the same as the man who'd hit my car.

The business section was a maze of tight shelving holding, among much else, all the government publications. Imprinted spines held such fascinating titles as *81st Congress, 2D, 1909-1910, Senate Documents Volume 87, Congressional Record*. Journals were kept in white covers. Row after row, six shelves high, marched in formation down the room. The library was newly built and bright, but even so, amid what seemed like miles of closely packed shelves, I was beginning to feel claustrophobic. I tried to peer over the books to other aisles searching for anything moving but, for the moment, I seemed to be alone. I was still looking when I backed around the corner and bumped hard into the tail.

He was about six two and sloppy in the middle. His dull red hair hung in long, oily fronds around a thick neck and surrounded eyes set deep behind protruding cheekbones. America's answer to Genghis Khan. He looked mean as a tornado.

He didn't say a word, just stared like the gang members I'd seen on Court TV, daring me to make a move. He raised his head and a vicious smile began to spread. The idea of accusing him of following me was too idiotic to consider. Of course he was following me, and he wanted me to know it. I started to back away, wondering what to do next. The stacks may have been empty of other people at this hour of the afternoon, but the building itself was hardly unoccupied. Somewhere people were talking to librarians, searching through microfiche files, chewing their cuticles. I was almost as paralyzed as Bambi at rush hour, but I could hear voices at a distance. Summoning up an atypical strength of resolve, I broke from his stare and turned my head to seek a rescuer. Then I tried to scream.

Mistake.

Suddenly I was as tall as the top shelf and flying. The Tornado had hurled me against the bookcases as easily as if he were tossing a stick to his pit bull. When I remembered the sensation later, I was amazed at how long it seemed to take before I hit the floor. A stop-action film, it was made memorable by a blur of neon ceiling fixtures, mutely patterned carpeting and a million books.

I landed on my hip and shoulder, too stunned to do anything but watch as he dumped the contents of my purse into a brown paper bag which he then stuffed into one of his inside pockets. He watched me watching him with no expression whatever. Taking all the time in the world, he felt around the bottom of the now-empty bag with one finger. Obviously, he wanted more than money. Why wasn't someone coming? Didn't anyone hear me fall? Finding nothing more, he tossed the empty bag on my stomach. Too bulky to take with him, I guessed.

"We told you to back off, lady," he snarled, landing a kick on my thigh. "Next time it's for keeps." Now I did scream, and hard. He backed around another shelf and was gone.

I made a tentative move to sit up, mentally feeling each limb for breaks. I seemed whole. By the time someone with a library badge found me still on the floor, a good five minutes had passed. The room was set off from the main area with its desk of librarians. The pleasant-faced young man choked slightly when he saw me, turning the sound as best he could into a cough.

"Gee, what happened? Are you all right? We thought we heard a thump back here, but the phones were ringing. Did you fall?"

I told him the basics, leaving out the fact that I'd been followed. He hoisted me up and took me to a table with empty chairs. Then he left me there while he went for help. I took a perfunctory look for the green jacket but I knew the guy was long gone. I was going to have some spectacular bruises, and it was already becoming clear where they were going to be. My head buzzed. Everything in the room seemed vague. I forced myself to concentrate on the contents of my purse but I was only half successful. At least my car was in the shop. The keys the creep got would only fit the rental. I'd have to call the company and have them check the parking garage back at the hotel where I'd left the car. What else was there? Phone numbers? I think I was still walking around with Hallie's, which I'd finally written down. Mailin's new address. House keys? Yes, alas. My first move would be to have the locks changed. Today. I needed my husband. It wasn't fair to ask someone as traumatized as I was to think. I covered the ground to the main desk and called Albert, taking the chance he might still be in his old office. He was. He promised to be right over. Even so, right over meant half an hour at least even if he tried for warp speed. I called off the library people who were trying to find me a doctor, and thanked them for their help.

No one had disturbed the papers I'd found before Magda had shown up. I'd located a fair number of pieces on radiation sickness, printing out what I could download from the computer. My whole body had started stiffening up. I needed some of those nonsteroidals Parker made, but there was no way I'd let anyone but Albert prescribe for me. With nothing else to do while I waited, I took a look at the fistful of pages. Sentences bounced around disconnected. Plutonium 239 was the world's most expensive substance. The tiniest amount near the skin could result in instant cancer. A sliver of radioactive cesium found in a home in eastern Europe killed a man and his dog and sickened everyone else. In the 1920s, the men who painted glow-in-the-dark radium faces on watches began to suffer awful facial cancers. It seems they liked to lick the brush to sharpen the point. Large shipments of very hot materials were being sent from parts of the old U.S.S.R. to the United States, requiring great care in packaging and handling. My head was starting to hurt. A lot.

I knew I'd found something more on radiation. Frightened and sore as I was, I couldn't stop hunting for answers, not when I'd bothered to dig up information. Besides, I wouldn't give that creep the satisfaction of derailing me. After shuffling through every scrap of paper, I spotted the journal article on the floor by the aisle. The pictures were horrifying. People who had been caught in nuclear accidents, even some old photos of Hiroshima. Humans who looked as red and crackled as hard candy. I left that and everything else behind. I'd learned enough for now, in every way.

By the time of the afternoon network news, I had been probed, checked over, and put to bed with ice packs. Millie was in her element, caring for me in exactly the same way she'd helped me ride out measles and chicken pox thirty years before. Toast and hot chocolate on the bedside table. Albert, to be companionable, had brought his pepper vodka upstairs and was on the bed beside me watching the news. Once Millie left the room, I took the glass from him and swigged a therapeutic dose. As far as Millie and the rest of the world was concerned, I'd been mugged. Purse stolen. Detective Morrisey had been told the truth and was planning to come talk to me around dinnertime.

When the phone rang, we were sure it was Morrisey canceling. It was, in fact, Parker LeMay. Albert had taken the call so I didn't know what had transpired till he'd hung up. I was too busy trying to get comfortable with an ice pack on one hip to bother eavesdropping.

"Well, it seems our erstwhile co-owner would like to see us."

"Really? What did he say?"

"There are some things he wants to tell us. Things that are weighing on his conscience. He sounded like he may have been drinking, actually. I keep thinking of him alone in that huge loft. Anyway, I told him we'd call as soon as we got back from flying, toward noon tomorrow. Hey, are you going to be all right for that?"

"I'm never all right for that."

"For flying, I mean."

"I know what you mean. You looked worse than this when you had that fall on the slopes at Alta. I'll be okay to fly, as long as you dope me up a little. In fact, I may like flying dopey so much, I'll never do it any other way. Do you think Parker's going to tell us he killed his wife?"

"No. Great Scott, woman! He's going to tell us that Trisha Potts's death was his fault. Maybe we should go over there now."

"Now!" I took the ice pack from my hip and threw it, Michael Jordan style, into the wastebasket, a perfect hit. "Here I'm mortally wounded, and all I get for this self-sacrifice is that you want me to get up from my bed and go downtown now? Forget it." I flipped onto my stomach and pulled the blankets over my head, burrowing down. "I'm finished till tomorrow."

As it turned out, that decision was my second big mistake of the day.

FOURTEEN

NIGHTMARES KEPT waking me, the darkness held new terrors, and I couldn't lie still. I thrashed until the blankets ended up on the floor at the foot of the bed. The warmth of Millie's flannel nightgown must have overwhelmed me and I'd stripped it off. It ended up in a floral heap on the chair. Somewhere in the middle of the night, Albert had sat me up and handed me painkillers and a glass of water. They'd helped. Both of us had then been able to doze off for a while.

What I saw the next morning in the full-length mirror on the bathroom door was just plain ugly. Big bruises covered my right upper arm and my thigh almost to the knee. I had cuts on one ankle plus the sharp, dark place on the other thigh where the kick had landed. My face had survived with only a dark strip under the jawline when a shelf edge caught me as I fell. A sane person might have taken all this as some kind of message.

Even Detective Morrisey seemed a tad disturbed. He asked for and got a complete description of the Tornado, but I could tell it wasn't ringing any bells. He'd waited with us till an emergency locksmith had come and done at least a temporary change of all the locks in the house. Since he was technically off duty, he joined Albert in a glass of Mexican beer while he recorded everything I could think of that had been in my purse. I could tell that my having Mailin's address and Hallie's number in there concerned him. It concerned me, too. If something bad happened to either of them, Mailin or the mystery woman, I'd consider it my stupidity. I groaned, thinking of all the calls I'd have to make canceling and replacing cards and licenses. The rental car company had succeeded in finding their car in the hotel lot. They promised to bring me another one by afternoon. Apparently, the goon didn't care enough to go through the whole place matching license plates to the keys he had. But then again, why should he? His intention was to scare me off, and he'd come close. He'd scared me, all right. No question. Just not off.

Despite the long-sleeved shirt and slacks I'd put on in the morning to cover the worst of the marks, the twins saw right away that something had happened. Their eyes went wide. Spence couldn't talk at all and Paul could only say again and again, "Mom. Mom." To my mortification, tears filled my eyes. We all stood huddled together beside the table, arms under, around, and over each other. Even Albert joined the touching scene. I could only hope that in years to come, when the boys went over their early years with their therapists, they would remember such moments.

It had been a week since Jann died, and still we weren't much closer to knowing the true story. I only hoped we could discover the murderer before something more serious happened to me or, heaven forfend, to any of us.

Millie had been unusually grim as she served breakfast. After the twins had left for school, she sat down beside me on an empty chair. At moments like this, neither of us bothered with any illusions about our relationship. We reverted to mother hen and chick, my childhood make-believe with her. She checked the bruise under my jaw and whatever cuts she could find, probing like a school nurse. "All right," she said finally, sitting back. "We're not going to tell your mother anything about this, this…mugging. I won't say anything, and you're not to say anything. She sounded a little depressed to me yesterday. We don't need to give her anything to worry about." Automatically, she folded napkins and collected the nearby glasses. "But I want you to know I don't think this and that car business are just…things that happened. So you watch out, miss. You have kids now." She stood and began to clear the table, still frowning. "You're not a crazy ten-year-old anymore."

I knew what she was thinking. When I was ten, I had decided it would be fun to hitch a ride to the next small oil town, buy some magazines and comics, and hitch a ride back before anyone could tell I'd been gone. It worked halfway. A truck had taken me safely to my destination, a dusty one-street village which boasted one very well-stocked drugstore. I'd had a fine time reading in the back of the shop where no one bothered me, working my way through all of the romance comics I wouldn't have dared bring home. It was great fun till late afternoon when my stomach began to rumble. Time to go home for dinner. The trouble was, I couldn't find a ride back. By nightfall, my hysterical parents and Millie had found me trying to walk home, a distance of twenty miles down a lonely road. My mother, whose memory these days was not all it used to be, had probably forgotten this transgression. Millie never would. I never would either, though for different reasons. Scared as I was being alone in that strange town, I loved the feeling of independence and daring. Once my father had been killed, those days of freedom had ended, essentially forever. I'd had to grow up fast for my mother's sake. From then on, the neat endings promised by the literature of comic books eluded me. Oil well explosions, for example, don't leave a lot of pieces to bury. The only thing ever really brought to completion after that was my childhood.

I sat at the table nursing the last of my coffee, mulling old grievances and putting off the inevitable. I was obviously in no position to complain about flying. Right after breakfast, we took off for the airport where a rental plane was waiting for us.

Before claiming the plane, we stopped at the old hangar to pick up the books on *Sweet Juliet*. Albert seemed to think he could tell at least the radius of the LeMays' flights by the gas used and their time in the air. He chatted easily with Jack Potts who, after recovering from the shock of my appearance, seemed in better spirits than he had when last we met. I wanted to ask Jack about his sister, did he think it possible that she might have had radiation poisoning, but thought better of it. He almost certainly wouldn't know, and the question would just upset him. And Albert would have had a fit. Besides, the husband had happier things in mind. Apparently, he'd committed to buying the Turbo Arrow from Ohio, and plans were being made to deliver it. Jack Potts would be in charge of looking it over critically when it came, making sure everything was as advertised and working perfectly. Then, alas, we'd have to take it up for the first time. That would be even worse than the initial flight after an annual.

The rental was waiting patiently for us on the ramp. Albert did all the outside things, checking the gas, removing the chocks, poking and prodding, and then jumped neatly in, crawling through to the left seat. I patted the fuselage, my little superstitious ritual, then walked around to step delicately from footbar to wing. Once into the plane, there was so much to do. Seat belts, radio headsets, notes, clipboards. Whole lists of routines existed both in Albert's head and on paper. He'd tried repeatedly to get me to learn to use the radios, at least, but I refused. I needed all the control I had just to survive.

After the shout of ''Clear!'' and a go-ahead from the tower, we taxied to the assigned runway, received a clearance for takeoff, and were in due course airborne. The ground dropped away and spread for miles before us, a wonderland of cultivated fields and country roads winding toward the horizon. Flight was most surely an out-and-out miracle, best appreciated from a small plane. Some metal, a wholly inadequate little engine, and one left the earth behind. Amazing. Of course, it wasn't really necessary to *do* it. A video would have been fine.

Once airborne, Albert handed me a small ring notebook. "Here, would you keep track of this? Parker and I always jotted down the reading on the Hobbs meter so we knew how to divide the expenses and, luckily, we left the record in the hangar. Otherwise, it would have gone down with the plane. Now maybe we can figure out where he flew."

We headed west into the mountains, so breathtaking in the early-morning sun. The weather was keeping any turbulence, my absolute bete noire, away for the moment, so I managed to enjoy the sensation of becoming one with the mountains. Albert was scanning the ground carefully, checking the Hobbs, then the notebook. "There," he said, thirty minutes into the flight, pointing to an area between several major peaks. "That's roughly where Jann went down."

The crash site, viewed from above, seemed to have no flat space at all. No one could possibly have landed a plane in that small area, no matter how great the pilot's expertise. Albert dipped the left wing and began to fly in a spiral pattern, tracing wider and wider circles using the crash site as epicenter. "According to most of Parker's Hobbs entries into the notebook, his destinations could correspond to this area," he said. "What we're looking for is someplace near here that he or Jann might have landed intentionally."

"An airport? Hiding in the mountains?"

"Hiding a real runway would be practically impossible. You'd need a ground crew just to cover it after each use. What we're looking for is some place a plane could, if necessary, go down safely. And, of course, take off from again. But it's not likely to be a real runway." He checked the compass heading and corrected slightly. "I never really noticed before, but the notebook we keep seems to show about the same distance every time the LeMays logged on. And since we know Jann was heading in this direction at least the final time, well...I don't know. Just keep your eyes open."

I was not enjoying this circling maneuver at all. When my wing was the one lowered, seat belts or no, it felt like I was going to slide out of the plane. The last thing I wanted to do was stare down to check the topography, but I forced myself. The mountains here were broken and erratic, striking geologic formations that seemed to have slipped from their moorings and skidded down a gully. It was almost impossible to see the land at the bottom until we were directly overhead. Then it suddenly appeared. I'd almost given up and was longing for the plane to right.

"Look," I said. "Over there." Albert brought the plane to its level position and banked again, lowering his side to see where I was pointing. "It's a sort of abandoned highway."

It looked like a two-lane road that had been built originally to service a mining camp, then paved, maybe with the quixotic idea of attracting high-country tourists. It ran surprisingly straight across the flat of an unexpected plateau and then dropped off abruptly at the steepest edge. The idealist who planned it seemed to have run out of money and hope simultaneously. The road just quit. Albert, keeping an eye on the altimeter, turned to follow it back to its beginnings. He was holding the plane high to stay above the peaks and give us room to drop if necessary. My body by now was starting to feel gravitationally challenged. Hulking mountains rose on both sides of the mesa, forcing our little rental into tighter and tighter turns. If the stall horn had gone off during one of them, I would have simply had a coronary on the spot. Albert, into the zone, wouldn't have noticed I was dead for at least twenty minutes.

"Over there," he said, pointing. "What do you think that is?"

I forced myself to open my eyes, squeezed shut during the last dip. From the air, the structures Albert had singled out seemed to be the remains of old cabins, the type used by the area's miners early in the century. Weatherbeaten pitched roofs, now largely destroyed, covered the few shacks, all of which had long since gone off of square. Miners, those masters of temporary lodgings, didn't bother with foundations in soil so inhospitable. All they asked was shelter from the wind and cold, and they'd worry about next year next year.

"I think that's an old ghost town," I said.

"No, I mean that thing sticking out of one of the cabins. There, behind that stand of brush."

I saw where he was looking. "I have no idea. We'd need binoculars from here."

"Hold on. I'm going to take it down."

I wasn't scared. I was paralyzed. If we survived this idiocy, I was never never ever going to go up in a small plane again, but I wasn't about to distract the pilot at this moment by telling him that. He was already dropping.

At about a thousand feet above ground, we saw the hood of the truck. Someone, it seemed, had stashed a small pickup inside the remains of an old miner's hut. It didn't fit in all the way, the rear had been backed into some evergreen shrubs which partially covered it, but from a reasonable altitude, which meant at least five thousand feet higher than we were at the moment, no one would have noticed.

"A truck. I'll be darned." Albert added power, pulled up the nose, and we started our way through a pass between two peaks and out of the valley of the shadow of death. "And there," he added as we climbed, "is a gate. A sign there would keep any misguided automobile from using the road." I opened my eyes just a slit, enough to register the barrier below. Then I closed them again and tried to will blood back into my brain.

"I'll bet they've been landing our plane on that road. The whole thing fits. It matches the Hobbs meter distance exactly and is close enough to where Jann went down that she could easily have been heading there." He looked over at me hopefully. "Want to try landing there? Just to prove it can be done?" I was so appalled at the thought, all I could do was stare. "No, I guess not," said Albert quickly. "We'll just head back."

Once out of the highest mountains and back at a reasonable altitude, my anxieties, on a scale of one to a hundred, dropped down to a workable eighty-five. The blood returned from my feet. Finally I could talk again. "That's pretty amazing, isn't it? It's almost like they were flying to that mountain valley, landing on an abandoned auto road, and then taking some kind of truck or four-wheel-drive out of there. You think?"

Albert was wiping his forehead with a sleeve. I had a feeling he was experiencing flashback jitters now that the valley adventure was over. "They probably just drove that truck to the barrier, lifted it, and went back to the main highway. All sorts of small country roads peel out of there. They could have been picking something up. Ditching something. Having a picnic. Whatever they did, they could head back to the valley, replace the barrier, and hide the truck again. Then, they could turn the plane. It looked like there was room. A short-field takeoff. It's certainly possible."

"What if someone saw the plane on the ground?"

"What if? They might think the road was a privately owned airstrip. Besides, how long do you suppose they stayed there with the plane? I'd bet not very. The odds of being spotted would have been tiny."

"Are you going to ask Parker about this when you see him?"

"You might say that." He looked grim. "My list

of questions for Parker has just grown geometrically.''

Parker, however, was not available. Once back from the airport and home, Albert tried both the business and the loft with no success. His office said they had expected Mr. LeMay several hours earlier but he wasn't in. Should be any minute. LaShawn answered at the loft and said he'd left before she arrived. Was his car still in the garage? LaShawn didn't know and didn't have time to look. She was going to be late for her class if she didn't leave right then. We decided to go down and check the garage ourselves in a little bit, see if maybe he'd returned home, after we'd had some time to recoup from the morning.

I went to our room to change bandages and clothes. My stomach was still a little dicey after the wild ride. I couldn't think about lunch, though I heard Albert in the kitchen with Millie checking available options. Finally, partially refreshed, we headed downtown in Albert's Grand Cherokee. The rental company would have a car for me by afternoon, and we could pick it up after talking to Parker.

We had a lot to talk about.

FIFTEEN

WE FOUND A PLACE on the street near the loft.
Lunchtime crowds were filling the adjacent side-
walks as we walked by, but the area by the loft itself
was empty. The building had one of those fancy
call-box entry systems. It didn't respond when Albert tried the LeMays' number. The adjacent garage
could only be approached from an inside entrance,
and we were trying to figure out how to access it
when a uniformed UPS driver emerged from the
front door and rushed to his truck without a backward look. We were planning to try all the numbers
till we could find someone to let us in but this was
easier. We pushed against the massively heavy door
before it could shut and found ourselves in a small
brick-walled lobby. Several benches and chairs
clung tight to the sides of the room, giving what
little space there was a bit more importance. The
sign just to the right near the front said garage.

Once through the door, it became obvious that,
for the second time that day, we didn't know exactly
what we were looking for. No more than half a
dozen cars remained in the parking structure, which
was fortunate since we didn't know what Parker
drove. We wandered around somewhat aimlessly,
looking into car windows for clues. Most of the cars
were decidedly upscale, matching the expense and

sophistication of the building. I prayed that no one
would come down to take her Lexus or BMW out
shopping, drive away, and call 911 from a cell
phone to report intruders. Albert seemed calm
enough but atypically at a loss. For want of a better
idea, he began recording license plate numbers on
the back of a check stub. Maybe, he suggested, it
would be worth running them by Parker's personal
secretary for a match.

The last car, a metallic turquoise Volvo, had the
furthest space in the southwest corner. The ceiling
bulb in that area seemed to have burned out, casting
the area in shadow. We strolled over without much
enthusiasm, certain that we were about to bomb out
on this idea.

The body was slumped sideways across the front
seat. A small pool of blood had formed under the
right ear and was seeping into the crack between the
leather sections. The bullet's exit wound seemed to
be over and slightly above the left eyebrow where
Parker's biologic defenses had made a last-ditch effort to clot the flow of blood. He was dressed in a
jacket and tie, his white shirt unspattered. He looked
as if he could sit up, brush himself off, put a bandage over the hole in his forehead, and step into a
board meeting except for one small thing. He was
very dead.

I gasped and started back away from the window.
"Oh, what— My God! Albert."

Albert stared at the figure in the car for a long
minute, considering. Then he said, "Is the phone in
your purse?"

Half the time, I forget to carry it, but this time I had it with me. I handed it to him and he called Morrisey from the garage. While he was talking, I walked around to the passenger side and peered through the glass. Parker's right hand, hanging over the seat edge, seemed to be holding a gun, but I couldn't be sure in the dim light. I'd been too schooled in television-produced police procedure to touch the handle, but too experienced as a reporter not to want to. A suicide. Was there a note?

The guilt took no time at all to set in. Suicides do that to people left behind, even if they aren't directly involved. If we'd really come over to see him last night, could we have prevented this? Or did we in fact cause it? Were we beginning to ask him all the wrong questions? The idea that we, far from being uninvolved, might have caused this was too horrible. I walked away from the car, almost slipping over some broken glass on the garage floor. I tried to stop shaking.

Albert folded the phone and put it back in my purse. "Come on," he said, taking my arm. "Let's wait for the police outside."

We felt around my bag, settling on a package of pocket tissues, and used it to keep the lock on the front door from shooting home. Then we went outside to wait, setting ourselves down heavily on a decorative stone block near the entrance. Comfort was impossible. The air smelled faintly urban, a mix of exhaust and food from nearby restaurants. Yesterday, I'd been hurled through the air at the library.

This morning, we'd dive-bombed into a mountain valley. My right shoulder ached and one deep scratch was itching under its bandage. And Parker was dead. I felt lousy. "It just keeps getting worse." I sighed. "Is this ever going to end?"

Albert, grim, shook his head.

Detective Munz, the tall one, arrived first with several other men. I decided he looked exactly like Raymond Massey playing Lincoln in the old movie.

He looked uncomfortable having to speak. "Would you two, um, mind waiting here? For Detective Morrisey? While we go in? To the garage?"

"Of course not. Please." I nodded toward the garage door.

Albert gave them the instructions to the car since I wasn't fully functioning. Morrisey arrived alone moments later in his own car, double parked easily, and apologized for being late. We briefed him on the morning, not including our airborne discoveries. Just the cruise through the garage and why we'd been making it, looking for Parker who was missing.

The detective listened carefully, nodding. Then he said, "I'd appreciate it if you'd wait out here." His voice was soft, polite. "I'm sure we'll have some questions for you. Are you comfortable?" He was looking at me, reassessing the bruises and bandages.

Across the street and down a quarter block I could see the sign for a middle-eastern restaurant, apparently open for lunch. It looked warmly inviting, even from the outside. "No, in fact, I'm not. Could we meet you down there?" I asked, nodding at the ornate sign. "A cup of tea actually sounds good to me. That's how far gone I am."

Morrisey agreed. After watching him disappear into the building, we walked with our own thoughts down past antique shops and galleries to the cafe. The lunch crowd was largely gone, leaving a number of uncleared tables and residual smells of odd spices. I looked around at the still-remaining customers, wondering if any of them had known Parker and would be as shocked as we were to know what had happened to him. He must have come here now and then for a meal, or maybe just a drink with Jann. It was so close, and what was the point of downtown living if one couldn't enjoy ethnic restaurants and night spots easily? We asked for a table for four and, when one was cleared, ordered. I couldn't go through with the idea of tea and when I saw on the menu the wonderful flavored buttermilk we'd had in India, I jumped at it. Albert did, in fact, order an English tea. Now and then I had to remind myself that he grew up in the east.

"We'll never know, will we," he said. "All the answers are gone now." He looked beat. Even his movements were slow.

"Suicide could be a confession," I said. "Parker must have arranged the 'accident' that killed Jann."

Albert shook his head. "I simply cannot believe that. And I can't believe either of them was involved romantically with anyone else, despite your suspicions. Everything we've ever heard about those two was about their devotion. He loved her too much.

Maybe he didn't find life worth living without her. Isn't that just as good a reason for suicide?''

"I guess. But I find *that* very hard to believe. He had too much still going on in his life."

"It really grinds me that we're not going to find out if that truck on the road was theirs and what they were doing with it. Darn!"

"And I want to know what was really going on with Mailin and where she got all those little baubles. And about Hallie Whozit."

Morrisey showed up, two buttermilks, three teas, and forty-five minutes later. We had managed to work ourselves into a major funk.

The detective pulled over a chair, sank heavily into it, and ordered a Turkish coffee. He seemed too weary to play games, only waiting till the coffee arrived to open up. "He's been dead a long time. Probably happened sometime in the middle of the night. The only reason no one saw the body sooner is that it was slumped over on the seat. You'd have to look directly in the car. And the light above the car wasn't working. He would have been there a lot longer if you hadn't gone snooping."

"Suicide?"

"Looks like it, but maybe not. We'll have to do some tests. Ask around. Munz and some of the others are up in his place now. Maybe they'll find something. When did you last talk to him?"

Albert answered that one. "Yesterday. He called last night. Sounded like he'd been drinking and he wanted to talk to me. I may spend the rest of my life wondering what would have happened if I'd gone over there right away."

"Did you hear anything in the background when you were talking to him?"

Albert frowned. "Just him. Though…"

"What?"

"Now that you mention it, there may have been a knocking. Someone at the door. Or the TV. Or he was tapping something. Like that." He rapped his water glass three times against the dark wood table. Water sloshed over, making a pool near his cup.

"Any idea why he wanted to talk to you?"

"Guilt," I cut in. "Albert suspected that Trisha Potts, a friend's sister, had been poisoned by radiation. He'd figured it out, about the pig. He told Parker and Parker obviously knew, well…I don't really know what he knew," I finished lamely.

"If nothing else, that he was guilty of putting his workers in jeopardy," Albert continued. "Or dealing with some kind of illicit material."

Morrisey seemed to be in a trance. He had to cough slightly before he could speak. "It's possible. It's all possible."

"Did you ever ask him what *he* was doing Thursday night?"

"Yes. He said he was home with Jann. Which, of course, we could hardly check out."

The restaurant door opened to a waft of cold breeze and Munz entered, vaguely disoriented by the darkness. He spotted us and hurried over. "We have something we think you should see, sir," he said. "Could you come back over to the scene?"

Morrisey pushed back from the table, standing up a little stiffly. He stretched his spine, arching backward before he looked at us. "Wanna come? You're pretty involved in all of this now."

I was on my feet. "Yes, absolutely." I hoped my husband wasn't planning to get any work done today because it wasn't going to happen. Even he would have to admit that this death took priority.

We trooped behind the stately Munz into the front hall of LeMay's building. Additional police cars were now parked outside and a stream of men seemed to be coming and going around the garage. A uniformed policeman was holding a plastic bag containing what seemed to be a small wrinkled card. "We found this in the deceased's hand," said Munz, offering it to Morrisey. "It's a business card for someone named Nicholas Qualls."

Albert and I immediately exchanged charged looks. Morrisey caught them. "You know this man?"

"We've met him."

The detective studied the card, not removing it from the bag. "You say you found this in his hand?" he quizzed Munz. "Which hand?"

"Left."

"And the gun?"

"In his right hand. It's been fired. The trajectory is congruent with a self-inflicted wound. We'll have to check, of course, to see if the bullet matches. It went clear through his head. We found it imbedded in the inside of the roof of the car."

"Was the deceased right-handed?"

Munz was taken aback. "Well, I don't know, sir. We haven't checked that out."

Morrisey looked at us. "Would you know?"

We both shook our heads. "No."

"Who's his closest relative? Any idea?"

I looked at Albert. "Mailin?"

"Beats me."

I turned to the detective. "Mailin Duong was…is his wife's sister. I had her address in the purse that was stolen, but I remember it, since it was such a surprise, her moving there." I told Morrisey the name of the residential hotel. "She's the only one I know of that's related."

Morrisey pulled Munz aside and spoke directly into his ear. The younger man hurried out. After a moment, we heard a car door slam.

Morrisey returned to us. "We're going to try to find Miss Duong. Would you mind waiting here for her? You two seem to be the only people with any interest in the deceased. The men seem to be finding that basically no one in the building knows him."

We found one of the ornate benches in the lobby and sat down. Both of us were beginning to feel punchy. I wondered if the boys were home from school yet, if Spence had been chastised for the blackjack game, or if he'd even been caught with it. I was beginning to long for normalcy.

The door flying open gave me a serious start. Mailin rushed past us into the garage. Munz was right behind her, trying to talk her into waiting for someone to accompany her. Her high-pitched, anxious voice echoed through the closing door. And then a wail, long and keening, dissolved to a whimper when the heavy steel panel closed. A sister and brother-in-law violently dead in a single week.

Twenty minutes later, Mailin returned to the lobby, still crying. Munz had a stoic arm around her shoulder. We stood to make room for her to sit. She took the seat without registering us at all. Morrisey arrived, emerging from the steel-cased elevator. He sat down quietly, waiting for her to regain her composure.

"I'm so sorry, Miss Duong. I know how hard this must be for you. I would like to ask just a couple questions if you think you're up to answering them."

Mailin nodded and found a tissue to blow her nose. I noticed she'd changed to a larger purse with a zipper since the spill in the hotel lobby.

"Did you have any reason to believe your brother-in-law was suicidal when last you saw him?"

"No. He seem, you know, jumpy, but he always seem jumpy. Parker a nervous man."

"When did you last see him?"

"Last night." Her eyes widened in remembrance. "Just last night."

"And he seemed to you in no way abnormal?"

"No."

"Did you come here to his loft?"

She nodded.

"And, if I may ask, what was the nature of your visit?"

"Huh?"

"Why were you here?" Morrisey's voice had acquired just the tiniest bit of an edge.

"I come to pick up money he give me. He owe me. He was as he was, you know? We did not get along so well."

The detective nodded. "Yes. Well…Detective Munz is going to ask you a few more things, perhaps upstairs if you don't mind."

Munz looked at her, impassive.

"Then we'll wait till you've had a chance to recover before talking to you further. In the meantime, don't leave town, okay?"

She nodded.

"Oh, incidentally, was Parker right-handed?"

"No, no. He left-handed. Always. I remember. It look so funny when he write my check."

No left-handed person would shoot himself above the right ear. Morrisey seemed galvanized by the answer. "All right," he said to Munz. "When you're through here, take Miss Duong home. And check her room before leaving her. And then, I want you to find Nicholas Qualls."

Exhausted, we nodded to Morrisey and let ourselves out the door. He barely acknowledged our leaving. Late-afternoon sunlight cast our long shadows on the street and the chill made our light jackets welcome as we headed for the Cherokee. Rush-hour traffic was picking up. The car was where we had left it. I remembered the last time I drove away from the LeMay loft and what had happened to my Aurora. I looked hard at Albert's wheels. They seemed untouched.

Albert edged the car into the serious traffic on the

highway and I sat back, totally wiped. I knew Millie had had a doctor's appointment this afternoon, so any messages would have been left on our machine. I pulled out the cell phone and dialed the access number for my messages. Only one, and it turned out to be from Beebee Ballard. "Hi, Gracie, it's me." She knew I'd recognize her voice and of course I did. "Just wanted to tell you that I've turned up some kinda nasty information on Nicholas Qualls. He seems to have some mob associations. Was indicted for fraud several years ago. The case is still pending. People tell me he's a man best kept away from. I'd take that bit of advice seriously. There's a little more, but it's in the same vein. I'll tell you Tuesday when I see you or, if you want, call me back. Hope you're okay. 'Bye."

I pushed END, and reported to Albert. "Beebee. She says Qualls is a crook. Basically."

His expression implied this was not hot news.

Then, since the phone was still in my hand, I dialed Hallie, a number I'd tried a dozen times, always getting the answering machine. The machine clicked and a voice, far more anxious than seductive, answered. "This is 555-1340. Please leave your message."

Up till now, I hadn't done anything but hang up. Not this time. "Hallie, this is Grace Beckmann. You don't know me, but I need to talk to you. I believe you're in danger. I'll call you in the morning."

No way would she refuse to speak to me now. And I wasn't lying. I could only hope she'd still be alive by morning.

SIXTEEN

SATURDAY MORNING and D-Day. Or PSAT Day. Paul came down to breakfast wearing his good-luck shirt, a gift from Albert's sister, Phyllis. The T-shirt commemorated one of the early Beatle tours and had been lovingly washed and packed away by its owner. Paul treasured it beyond life and wore it only on earth-shaking occasions. Like this morning. Spence, on the other hand, slouched into the breakfast room yawning, his all-black shirt and jeans impossibly crumpled.

"Full of vigor and drive, I see," I said to Spence. "When did you get to bed last night?"

"It was late," he admitted. "I got involved in this game on the Net. It just went on and on. Neither of us could win. But I did, finally."

"Great. I'm thrilled for you. Today, except for a little test you have to take this morning, you don't have much on the agenda. You'll be able to sack out and recover."

Spence smiled sleepily and reached for the juice. "Okay, Mom. I got the message."

Albert arrived, his eyes outlined by stress. He grinned when he saw Paul. "Oh, boy, Phyllis's Beatle shirt. I almost forgot, this is a five-star day. You guys ready?"

"Some more than others," I answered for them.

While Millie took Albert's request for two poached eggs on wheat toast, I went into the kitchen and emerged with my own good-luck talisman for the boys: two bags of M&Ms. I handed one to each of them with instructions. "Now feed these into your system throughout the morning. Leave the open bag in your pocket and just slip a few into your mouth every few minutes. They'll keep your blood sugar up and fend off fatigue. Promise?"

They nodded. "And I know," I lied, "you'll both do great." I hugged each of them as they headed out the door. Paul, who held the hug a little longer than usual, whispered in my ear just before leaving. "You're worried about the wrong person. But I'll try."

I sat at the table and dawdled even more than normal for a Saturday morning, waiting till I could respectably call Hallie. Albert was staring at a point somewhere to the left of the paper, pretending to read. I cleared my throat several times before he looked up.

"What?"

"You look distracted. Care to enlighten me?"

He sipped his coffee as a delaying tactic. Finally, "Yeah, well… Okay, something did happen. I didn't want to tell you, really, but…I suppose I might as well." He put his cup down carefully, centering it in the saucer depression. I waited.

"Ozzie Westgaard. You remember him?"

Of course I remembered him. The funeral. The fight with Parker at the airport. I just waited. And waited some more.

"I learned at the hospital yesterday that he's fled to Central America. In fact, Tony, my old flight instructor, flew him down himself. Or so I heard."

"So?"

"He's left a pretty good mess behind. Lost a lot of several wealthy clients' money. Seems to have dipped into some of the school funds, too. He had a limited power of attorney for some of our business."

I licked my finger and stabbed a toast crumb that had fallen to the table. "That's too bad. But why did you worry about telling me all this? It doesn't affect us, does it? Did you invest with him?"

"No. But I was in the process of catching him." Albert poured another cup from the vacuum carafe. "I see our department books now and then. Noticed a discrepancy. A pretty big one, so I asked around. The trail led to Ozzie. So a few, maybe six, weeks ago, I cornered him in the hospital cafeteria and asked him outright."

"And he denied everything."

"Not at all. Admitted it."

I felt, by turns, amazed and then uneasy. "What did he say, exactly?"

"That he'd made some investments with other people's money, including our school funds. That he knew he could replace the money, and would as soon as a big deal he was expecting went through. One of the investments he happened to mention was in Parker LeMay's company." Albert bit at a hangnail. I'd never seen him do that before. "I told him

I'd wait a limited amount of time and give him a chance.''

"You didn't say a word about this when you saw him at Parker's loft.''

"It didn't seem civilized in that setting.''

"And now he's split.''

"He must have thought the deal was going south for some reason. If he'd just held on, he could have waited for Qualls to merge, or whatever.''

"Maybe," I said. "You think he had some reason to want Parker dead? He was seen at the airport, according to Potts, but I don't see the logic.''

"No, not Parker, actually. It occurred to me that he had some reason to want *me* dead.''

I wanted to hit the table with my fist but didn't dare for fear of bringing Millie out to see what happened. "Terrific. Shouldn't we tell Morrisey about this?''

"I already have.''

One more biggie to worry about in my ever-growing litany of worries. For the first time, we discovered there was someone out there with at least some motivation for murdering us. Someone with a connection to Parker. Did he have an alibi for that infamous Thursday night? My mind was doing double axels.

I thought about all the things on my worry list, even without counting the events of the last week. Albert and his eggs and red meat, for example. He dutifully had his cholesterol checked at the hospital every year and never called for the results. And the boys, one who couldn't care less and one who cared too much. If I could only control their every waking moment, I could keep the world at bay for them. I was a little worried about the article I kept ignoring. I had a good relationship with this editor and I was jeopardizing it. As soon as all this was over, I'd tackle it, absolutely. And to top off all my problems, my bruises were spreading and had acquired a yellowish tinge this morning and I wasn't sure how successful I'd be at hiding them. Did I need to add to this litany by worrying about a woman I didn't know, had no last name for, and who may not fit in at all to the matters at hand? Yes. Yes I did.

At the stroke of nine, I dialed the number. The voice that answered seemed wary. "Hello?"

"Hello, Hallie, this is Grace Beckmann. I left a message on your machine yesterday."

"Yes. I got it. What do you want?"

I explained that her number had been in my purse and my purse had been stolen by someone she wouldn't like to know. Also, we knew she'd been involved in some way with Jann and Parker LeMay and they were now, as of yesterday, both dead. Her gasp told me the part about Parker was news. My husband and I wanted to meet with her if possible, I said, since we were afraid she might be in danger.

"You may be telling me this a little too late," she said, the softness of her voice now carrying overtones of fear. "I think my apartment was broken into yesterday. Nothing was missing, but someone was in here. I'm a little frightened."

She was reluctant to meet in her own place, now that it felt violated by an intruder, and she wouldn't consider meeting strangers in their house. We agreed the zoo would be safe, at a bench near the polar bear exhibits. I told her I'd find a yellow mum to wear in my lapel. There were still a few in bloom in the yard.

"By the way, Hallie, what is your last name?"

"McCullum. I have short blond hair. And it's not...well, completely natural."

Imagine apologizing for hair coloring. She sounded so naive, almost childlike. I hoped we could keep her, at least, from being hurt. We weren't exactly batting a thousand on that score.

Even though it was Saturday and a popular day for the zoo, the crowds were down. A thin sun did little to warm the air which, as Millie had predicted, was cool for October. A few weekend fathers drifted about with small children in tow, checking their watches. Kickoff for college games was two o'clock. The vegetation smelled of rotting leaves. Ever since the incident at the library, I found myself looking around for any hint of the Tornado. I did so now, scanning the group around the polar bear exhibit. At one time, a pair of particularly winsome cubs had had their fifteen minutes of fame, pulling hordes of viewers to their little corner, but they were long gone. Today only a handful of bear aficionados were left. The Tornado wasn't among them.

Hallie sat on a bench alone, long legs crossed. One look and the childlike image her voice had projected blew into a thousand pieces. Hallie McCullum, whose hair was most egregiously unnatural, was probably the most beautiful woman I'd ever been forced to admire. Full lips, a perfect nose, and eyes so blue I thought she must be wearing tinted contacts. I took a sideways peek at Albert, not a man on whom such beauty would be lost. His own eyes had gone unnaturally bright. A small black voice inside told me that no woman who looked that good needed anything from me, but I managed to send the black voice packing. Besides, it was too late now. She spotted the yellow mum and stood up.

"Hi," she said, hand outstretched. "I'm Hallie." She was as tall as Albert, with the body of an Isaac Mizrahi model, wearing various denim separates that would have looked great on a fourteen-year-old. I had never until this moment felt middle-aged. The gorgeous face, however, was creased with worry. "Is Parker really dead? That's just so hard to believe. Do you know what happened?"

"Maybe suicide," I said, "And maybe not. Not clear yet." I started walking before she could ask any more questions.

We found a place away from the main paths where two benches had been placed at angles and commandeered them for our own. No one seemed to be around. I decided to hit fast and hard.

"Hallie, the reason your phone number was in my stolen bag was that it had been on a memo in Jann LeMay's purse the day she died. Can you tell us why it was there?"

She was instantly defensive. "Are you lying to me, are you actually the press? Trying to make me trust you to get a story?"

Was I the press? Did freelancers qualify? I never really knew how to respond to that question, but in this case the answer was simple. "No. We were Parker's plane partners. We're just trying to find out what happened."

She was a study in conflicting emotions. She fidgeted, trying to get comfortable with the rough metal against exposed thighs. "After I talked to you this morning, I asked my...my husband what to do. He's very nervous, but he knows it's a murder investigation. He figured we probably would end up, well... As you probably guessed, our relationship is a secret. Once Jann was killed, I think we both knew we'd be involved eventually. He asked me to plead with you to keep whatever I'm going to tell you confidential. Just because you're good people and don't want to hurt anyone. Please? Can I trust you to do that?"

Her *husband?* Give me a break. This wasn't the kind of woman who padded down to the kitchen in a robe and made coffee. Besides, I didn't know what to say, since I couldn't be sure that whatever we learned might not someday become important. I hated promising what I might not be able to deliver. Fortunately, Albert answered for us. "We can keep any parts of your lives secret that have nothing to do with the murders. And the parts that are involved, well, we should be able to protect the source. Would that do it?"

She smiled and for the first time, relaxed a bit. Some women simply do better with men. When she returned Albert's look something, maybe the slightly artificial air, dropped away. "Gosh," she said, "we have nothing whatever to do with the murders. I know why Jann had my number, but no one would kill her for it. And if whoever broke into my apartment was looking for something to do with that, they didn't find it."

I was getting lost in the indefinite pronouns. "Okay then," I broke in, "let's start with why Jann LeMay would be carrying your phone number in her purse."

"Oh, that one's easy. Jann used to cover for us. All the time. After all, she worked for my husband. She knew all about his schedules and could find time for us to be together."

I sat back, stunned. Jann worked for the governor, who wasn't married. Or was he? Parker wasn't having an affair with Hallie. Jann wasn't having an affair with the governor. All those secrets that La-Shawn had suggested, all the times she'd surprised Jann and the governor whispering and lying, were something else altogether. Hallie was the governor's "other woman," the one Magda was talking about. The one, probably, in whose apartment he'd been caught. And Jann, loyal, upwardly mobile woman that she was, was their go-between. It was that simple, if you can call such devious behavior simple. But…her husband?

"Why would you have to worry about being with your 'husband'…if that's who he is?"

"Oh, that's who he is, all right. We were married on the q.t. in another state two years ago last April."

Her voice had developed an edge. "Yeah, I know he dated. But that was a cover."

I looked at her now more critically. The beauty was still there but altered, toughened. "Why the secrets?" I asked finally. "Why didn't he just introduce you to the public? Why all this mysterious nonsense?"

"I wouldn't have been accepted. Don't ask me why, please. I don't want to tell you."

We were all silent for a long minute before my intuition kicked in. Don't ask me how I knew. It was the one thing that made sense. "Prison?" I asked.

She nodded, her lips tight. Then, "Yeah, okay. You're right, though I can't believe you figured it out so quick." She was thoughtful, remembering. "Under the circumstances, we thought it best for me to stay in the background. He is a politician, after all. The press would have gone on a feeding frenzy. How many governors have a wife who did time for killing a guy when she was sixteen? Even when he deserved killing." She bent toward me, her loveliness accented by intensity. "Bob is the only strong man I've ever had in my life. We love each other and need to be together. I could have waited to marry, I didn't care. But he insisted." Her hand found my arm in an attempt to make me an ally. "His term is up in eighteen months. Then we don't care who knows about us anymore. He'll introduce me as his wife. Till then, though, it's just a lot easier not to."

It was easy to guess that her dazzling good looks

had worked against her here. And I could tell the cost to her pride the deception had taken. Modern politics can exact a terrible price.

Albert's knee brushed mine. I had to clear my throat. "Well, uh... Why do you suppose Parker was so careful to hide your number when he found it in Jann's things? Did he know about your... arrangement?"

Hallie pulled out a brown cigarette, tapping it once on her wrist but leaving it unlit. "Oh sure," she said, recrossing those incredible legs. "There were never any secrets between Parker and Jann. At least, not according to Bob." She seemed relieved to be able to use his name openly. "I used to tease him about having a thing for Jann himself. He said it would have been a complete waste of time. She was a one-man woman and Parker was the one man." She turned serious again. "It doesn't surprise me that Parker tried to protect us, even after Jann was dead. After all, he was the one who covered for us when I went to that conference in Eastern Europe with Bob, and that was plenty scary. That lasted a whole week, so we all had to work real hard to keep the press off the scent. Jann was just terrific, but so was Parker."

That old electric buzz sounded somewhere under my breastbone. There was something important here. What had I read about the federal government sending a few governors halfway around the world for a meeting?

Albert remembered the story first. "That was a little over two years ago, wasn't it?" he asked. "The papers considered it something of a boondoggle, as I recall.''

Hallie stiffened. "It was perfectly legit. They were looking at small countries that had just come out from Communism, giving them advice and stuff. Bob learned a lot from that. And gave a lot. Of course…'' She examined her hands. "Of course, my being there wasn't on the up and up, exactly, but I didn't go on the official plane. Bob paid my way on a commercial airline.''

"Did Jann go with him?'' I asked.

"He was allowed to take an assistant, and she wanted to go. She covered for us, so we could be together. I have no idea what she did with herself all the time Bob was at my hotel instead of working with her, if that's what you're asking. I imagine she did a lot of shopping.''

"Shopping? I wouldn't think there would have been much to buy then,'' I said. "Why do you think she went shopping?''

Hallie looked like the question was too foolish, even for me. "Because she came back with large boxes, that's why. Isn't that what people do when they've been shopping?''

Albert picked up the scent. "Any idea what she bought? Did you ask her?''

"Um, I think she said rugs. Lots of rugs. Whatever, Bob was able to take them back on the government plane so maybe she didn't have to pay duty. Immunity or something. I guess the weavers were sending them into Estonia from parts of Russia.''

"Oh, you were in Estonia?''

"Don't you read the papers?"

Albert grinned, throwing me the swiftest of glances. "Not very well," he said. Actually he memorized them both every morning. "But I suspect this trip was of more interest to you than it was to us."

"Yes. Well..." She sat up straighter. "Now I've told you all I know. Jann had my number in her purse and that's why. Is the you-know-what going to hit the fan, or are you going to be good guys?"

We assured her that we'd do the best we could to keep their relationship confidential. I cringed when I thought of all the misdirected gossip but I had really no reason to doubt her story. This confession, whatever else, had cleared up the question of why His Honorable had bothered to come himself to the gathering after the memorial service. He needed to look around, get some idea if anyone else was close enough to the LeMays to be in on Jann's confidences. For that, he couldn't send a surrogate.

We thanked Hallie who, like a schoolgirl released from the principal's office, took off with long, fast strides. Albert and I, still mulling over all we'd learned, remained on the bench, trying to incorporate the new information. In the distance, an animal bellowed, a lonely sound. Zoo animals must sense the coming of winter, hinted at even during these mellow fall days. Winter to them must mean about what it means to their keepers: more time spent indoors waiting for good times to roll around again. Do lions remember spring?

"So," I said, "what did you make of that?"

"I was particularly impressed with the boxes full of rugs, weren't you? Do you remember any Persians in her loft?"

I thought about the chrome and steel and hardwood floors. Here and there a rug was thrown, but I didn't remember any of the ornate, Oriental type. Mostly contemporary. Probably dyed to order. "Maybe she used them in her office. Or gave them away as gifts."

"Gifts to all the wonderful friends and family we know she didn't have?"

"Right. Okay, so what do *you* think she brought back?"

"How about contraband radioactive material? We know that stuff was bleeding out of Russia after the fall of Communism. And that a lot of it was coming through the Baltic states."

"Could she really have slipped all that through right under the governor's nose? Tricky."

"Think about it. Jann asked to go with the governor and he was certainly in no position to deny her anything. Not with everything she knew."

"She probably asked him if her boxes could go on the official plane where they might avoid scrutiny from customs people. He probably thought she was trying to save a few hundred dollars."

"Worth a try, anyway. And it must have worked. I'll bet she discovered a source for good-quality hot stuff that Parker needed in his business. A cheap source."

We lapsed back into silence. I broke it first. "Oh my God, Albert. It really works, doesn't it? Maybe they brought all that into the country and hid their stash in the mountains. Maybe she wasn't getting rid of hot waste the day she died, maybe she was picking up a new supply. That's why the pig was empty. But how, in those old Soviet Republics, did she know where to look for what she wanted? You don't just land in a foreign country with an arcane language and start asking around for illegal goods. She would have needed a source before she ever left the United States. She would have had to know what she was trying to do before she departed.''

''Mm-hmm. And there's a good chance we'll never have the answer to that, but keep in mind that Jann was a woman of the world. Literally. She still had connections in Asia. She had connections through the governor's office. She was not without resources.''

We were still speculating as we left the zoo, past elephants and stately elks. Years ago, we'd been here with the boys when two hippos had decided to consummate what had doubtless been a long-standing infatuation. The twins were certainly fascinated, as were we. Mating hippos *will* stop traffic.

Today, though, even that extraordinary sight wouldn't have slowed our forward motion. All our givens were in shreds, and urgency had replaced them.

SEVENTEEN

WE DECIDED to pick up my new rental car and call
Morrisey, probably in reverse order. Everything we
were thinking was pure guesswork except for the
story of Hallie and her very famous husband. Having given our word, all we could say was that Parker
LeMay was carrying her number for a reason that
had nothing whatever to do with anything illegal.
Secret, maybe, but not illegal.

Our car looked untouched. I walked clear around
the periphery, checking details, before I'd let Albert
even use his remote door opener. It seemed clean.

The sun, intensified by the car windows, made the
interior temperature considerably toastier than it had
been outside. We rolled down the front windows and
sat on the warm seats to plot strategy. Mailin was
the next person we had to catch. How much did she
know about Jann's European connections? When
last we'd seen her, she was dealing with Parker's
suicide/murder. The only time we'd really talked
was, as I'd come to think of it, the Day of the Jewelry. My questions then had been perfunctory. This
time I had new and different ones.

Eventually, Albert retrieved the cell phone and
dialed the police building. We got lucky. Morrisey,
whose phone produced only a voice mail recording,
answered his page. He listened quietly to all our

news and if there were a few obvious holes in our story, he chose to ignore them. Or so, at least, it seemed from my hearing only half the conversation. When Albert asked if anything new had happened since the disastrous events of yesterday, I could hear nothing beyond an occasional "hmm" or "interesting." He listened for long stretches, not even inserting a grunt of encouragement. The minute he hung up, I let him have it.

"So?"

"What?"

I shrugged. Albert turned the ignition and a few hardy sparrows, surprised by the sound, rose gracefully into the trees. As we headed toward the exit of the park, I glanced at the clock. "The boys must be about done with the test."

"Will they be coming home? I want to know how they did."

"As if they'd know. But they're not. They're celebrating with Tyler Oates and a couple of other kids. Going for pizza and a movie."

Suddenly, the idea of pizza sounded marvelous. Short on tomato sauce, lots of cheese, and toppings of onion, sausage, and mushrooms. Maybe even hot pepper flakes and anchovies. And I knew just where to find it.

We stopped at the rental place and picked up another of my tin lizzies, this one with cigarette butts in the ashtray. Three more days till the shop promised my Aurora back. We met at our favorite Italian café. It wasn't on any direct route from the zoo, but a real pizza urge is not to be denied. Each of us knew what the other was thinking and neither of us wanted to talk about it. Finished and feeling full and lethargic, we could put it off no longer.

Time to find Mailin. Yesterday, she hadn't even noticed we were there at the loft when she'd been brought in to see Parker's body. As if she hadn't been through enough, now we were going to use the excuse of her number being in my stolen purse as a reason to grill her ourselves. I went to retrieve my heavy sweater from the restaurant's coat rack up front and stopped short. On the next hook over hung a green jacket, size extra large. I looked around wildly but the place was dark. A very young girl, probably the owner's daughter, was carrying a pitcher of beer and four glasses into the adjoining room. Albert was still at our table, fishing out the tip. This was silly. Jackets like that were common.

I didn't say anything about the jacket to Albert. We left my rental in the restaurant parking lot, and headed toward the area south of downtown where Mailin had planned to set up her new digs.

The neighborhood was mixed but not without charm, a medley of three-story houses and newer high-rise apartments sharing zero lot lines. A building maybe sixty to eighty years old, the hotel had been recently purchased and vigorously redone by a society doyenne with both taste and money. The front portico was new and elegant, its facade covered with a slate-and-brass design. The dark crimson awning cried out for a liveried doorman, but if he did exist, he'd stepped out to lunch. We pushed our way through the heavy glass doors into the richly appointed lobby and came face-to-face with Mailin. She was standing quite near the door, surrounded by luggage. A phone dedicated, according to the sign, to a taxi company was in her hand. Five minutes later and we would have lost her, probably forever. The look on her face made it all too clear that she had planned it that way.

Before either of us could say a word, there was a rush of air on my back, then, "Were you planning to leave us, Miss Duong?" I turned in surprise. Detective Morrisey didn't look happy. He was accompanied by Munz, who, though temporarily distracted by the antique-style velvet chairs, was trying to look firm.

"Well, I guess I did sort of mention that we were thinking of coming over here this afternoon," Albert whispered. At least he had the good grace to look slightly embarrassed. I was trying to remember how he'd managed to convey this information. Some male-bonding intuition? Whatever, it was too late and there was nothing for it. There was an upside, though I hated to admit it even to myself. Granted, we'd lost the chance to interview Mailin privately, but we wouldn't have had the clout to keep her from simply walking out. The M&M boys, on the other hand, did.

Mailin, defeated, put back the phone. "Yes, I go someplace, but not now. Now you here."

"If you have plane reservations, perhaps you'd like to cancel them. We really would like you to remain in town for the time being." Morrisey never raised his voice. Still… Maybe I should sic him on Spence.

"No, no reservations. I hoping to get them at airport. It is time for me to go home." There was a mad, Anne Boleyn-to-the-executioners quality to her words. It was hard not to pity this woman.

The detectives arranged a bellman to return Mailin's bags to her newly abandoned suite, and we trooped along behind. Morrisey had already told Albert quietly that we would be allowed to stay in the room, and in fact, could ask whatever questions we had first.

All the rentals in this residential hotel were suites, not so opulent as the public rooms downstairs, but still pleasant and sunny. Flowered chintz and ticking were the dominant decorating scheme, well suited to a single woman of means, in this case with or without a discernible source of support. I sniffed the air for the same strange odor that had been in her room in Parker's loft, but here the air was sweet. Perhaps the hotel maids had done their work exceptionally well, or perhaps Mailin herself was in some critical way a changed woman. She had been in this country for a scant two years, just long enough, it seemed, to be corrupted by it. Now she had been planning to go home. Maybe she was in the process of returning to a purer state. I wanted to think so.

The men sat on the edges of the furniture. Chintz, it seemed, repelled them. I took the settee. Mailin chose a straight chair from the dining room table and sat with her ankles crossed. "All right," she said grimly. "What you want to know?"

Morrisey nodded to me. "You start."

Me? I had to regroup. "Well, for starters, did you know your sister and brother-in-law were dealing in illegal radioactive elements?"

She looked at me without expression. "Yes."

Well, so much for beating around the bush. "Did they tell you about it?"

"They could not have done it without me. I help them find source. In old country, I have, how you call, connections."

A rustle went through the room. "Weren't you afraid of being caught? Here you were in a foreign country. Weren't you afraid to be involved?"

"What did I do? No jail for giving a name. Jann went to get it. She in danger, maybe, not me."

Albert stepped in. "Did that have something to do with why you came to America?"

For the first time, Mailin changed positions ever so slightly. "I come here because I need to help get money. Parker's business going down then. They need my help. And my mother and me, we need money. Jann had always sent us."

"I know you didn't get along very well with Parker," I said. "Did he resent the fact that Jann sent money home?"

She looked down, her expression hard to read. "I resent. Me. Where I come from, family the most important. I here to help them, so why should *he* resent? I hate it here. I leave months ago, but then Jann ask me to stay. Why? I don't know. Maybe homesick. And then he send her in plane knowing she feel bad! I hate him. He kill her that way, and

I told him. I scream at him. She too sick to fly. Now too late. Now I go home.''

Jann was sick? I remembered Jack Potts saying she seemed, what, shaky? And LaShawn had mentioned something about her not being herself. But no one till now had said she was ailing. Even if she were, it wouldn't, as Mailin was saying, have caused her death. The plane was tampered with. Still, it was odd that Parker hadn't said a word about his wife's medical condition before the flight.

As for Mailin, the outburst was extraordinary for its vehemence. If I hadn't witnessed the scene after Jann's service, I wouldn't have realized how much fury was simmering in her. One wondered how Parker survived living with both Duong sisters, the two fire and ice. It was beginning to look as though it took both of them, though, to keep him solvent. Mailin, apparently, unearthed the scheme to bring in the hot cargo and Jann used her not inconsiderable wits and connections to find safe transport.

"Mailin..." It was Morrisey's turn. "Forgetting for the moment the tragic circumstances surrounding your sister's death, I need you to think about her husband. Do you think Parker really committed suicide?" He leaned forward, adding importance to the question. "When you last saw him, how did he seem to you?"

Her manner turned steely again. "He was fine." Period.

"When did you see him?"

"That night. The night you say he die."

"Was it you, perhaps, who knocked on his door

around eight-thirty or nine o'clock that night?'' asked Albert. "I thought I heard something when I was on the phone with him.''

"Yes. That me, I guess.''

"What were you doing there, Miss Duong?'' Morrisey was shifting into a higher gear. Munz wrote faster.

"I come to get a check. Big check. To take home with me to Vietnam. He give me half-million dollar. From Bio-Quest merger. That was the end, then. We can live on that forever. There not be any more.''

The detective's eyebrows rose a fraction of an inch. "Were you surprised at the size of the check?''

"No. And Parker okay. Usual. Not different.'' She stopped, apparently thinking about the answer. "Maybe a little more...serious. More...oh, I don't know.'' Her frustration with the language was obviously a tremendous hurdle.

I cleared my throat and cut in. "Did he mind giving you this big check?''

"Of course no,'' she said. "It for his own son.''

All four of us stared. A son? A son! If Mailin had announced that this pleasantly nondescript hotel room was really a time capsule and we were all currently on our way to the land beyond time, we couldn't have been more thunderstruck. The Le-Mays, this couple acknowledged by all who knew them as so single-mindedly devoted to each other that there was never any room for anyone else, had a child. But why had they denied his existence? I was there once when they'd been asked if they had children. Both had quickly answered no.

"The baby ring," I remembered softly. "The gold one with the design in your room..."

"Yes, that his. When he little. I bring it to Jann when I come, but couldn't find. I upset to lose it."

"But he isn't dead."

"No. I lied."

"And the jewels in your purse?"

"From Jann. For him. Good way to carry much money. Can hide."

She told us the story then. We listened with no interruptions. Her voice carried us to a time when survival itself was a matter of enormous skill, in a world gone mad with fear.

The girl that became Jann LeMay fell in love with the young Air Force pilot when she was just seventeen. The daughter of what, in more settled times, had been a highly regarded Saigon family, she had been warned by her parents to stay away from Americans. Her father had been a teacher of philosophy and religion with his own school, her mother a traditional wife. Both could imagine nothing good coming from the presence of foreign men in the city, particularly as regarded their two teenage girls.

The war had already forced the closing of the father's school. Income, and with it a sense of order, had become a problem. Eventually, the father would leave the city to find work teaching in the countryside, with the hope of sending money home until the time came when sanity returned, and they could resume their old life. As it happened, that was never to be. He disappeared, leaving his wife and daughters with barely enough to survive. They never knew what transpired and they continued to watch and hope even now, roughly a quarter-century later. The mother keeps her professor-husband's best silk clothes clean and hanging in a special corner, ready for the ceremonies that will surely take place when he reopens his school.

Nevertheless, the family unit held firm. Since obedience to parents was standard in those days, Jann had dutifully avoided the busier sections of Saigon where the foreign men hung out. As it happened, however, Parker LeMay had borrowed a bike from a native one day and set off by himself to see other parts of the city. The downtown bar scene, swinging day and night, had never interested the awkward kid, just barely into his twenties, who was, even then, very much an outsider. He was shy, in no way a romantic adventurer, and the fast city girls scared him. Jann and her friends, however, were a different story. They had been coming down a side street bringing small bags of vegetables and spices from the store for their mothers, and he thought he'd never seen such innocence and beauty.

Jann, even then, had gone her own way, at least so far as she could within the tight strictures of her society. The other girls, faced with an American who had stopped his bike and tried to amuse them with a few words of Vietnamese, grabbed their sacks, giggled, and ran home. Jann stayed. Had she sensed his insecurity and become protective? Had he appeared just as she was coming to terms with the idea that her father might never return? According to Mailin, who was a young teen at the time,

Parker was not unattractive, particularly in uniform. Whatever the reason, and despite parental warnings, the inevitable happened.

Jann had learned some English in school. Parker had picked up a few Vietnamese words, with their abrupt consonants and long, nasal vowels. Somehow, they found a way to communicate. She brought him home to show him off like a cricket in a cage, a particularly intriguing pet, and even her mother, after an original outburst of anger, found him charming. The whole family laughed as he tasted *nuoc mam,* the pungent fish oil sauce, and tried to pretend he liked it. They wondered at the hair on his body, stroking the brown curls on his forearms. So different, they agreed, from smooth-skinned Vietnamese men. Mailin offered to take him to a palm reader so he could find out when he'd be sent home. Both Jann and her mother worried about what the missing man of the house would think, but it was hard to remain too concerned in the face of his growing absence. Eventually, however, Parker was accepted by the now-reduced family. The young people had married and she was pregnant.

The baby's birth, when it came surrounded by chaos, was a disaster. The year was 1975 and the country then known as South Vietnam was falling to the communists. The streets of Saigon were frightening and dangerous. When it was time for Mailin to go for the midwife, she stayed close to buildings, sprinting the distances across roads, to avoid random shots. Once there, both Mailin and the midwife were trapped in the house by sounds of fighting outside. It was a long time, too long a time, before they could get back to the laboring girl.

The astrologer Jann had consulted about her pregnancy had seen something in the charts. They knew that. They had worried about Parker's exposure to the chemicals used for warfare, and with good reason. Sadly, the reality was worse even than they guessed. The baby was jammed in a partial breach position and without a midwife to turn it, there was nothing they could do. Jann, on her mother's bed, was in agony. By the time Mailin raced in with the woman who could help, both of them covered with the dust kicked off from the speeding army vehicles now throughout the city, the pinched cord had deprived the baby boy of critical oxygen. They never really knew whether it was that or Parker's damaged genes.

Whatever, at first, they hoped there'd been no harm done. A pretty baby, he was large, with his father's western eyes and his mother's thick, dark hair. He never cried. He held his arms stiffly to the side and resisted anyone moving them. His grandmother, the only one there with experience, knew things weren't right. She'd said later that she saw no reason to tell her daughters. They'd learn the truth soon enough.

Not long after, Saigon fell. C-130 cargo planes airlifted out those who had been on the American side, the planes often so crowded people were forced to stand through the entire flight. In the confusion of the last days, Parker was able to call in enough favors to get a spot on one of the planes for Jann.

She was torn, but pragmatic enough to accept the space. She promised her mother she'd be back for the baby, whom they'd named Howard after Parker's father, and at the time she'd surely meant it. Her mother, sad but serene, told her to go and Godspeed. Mailin would be there to help with the boy. They'd get along.

Jann never went back. She and Parker sent money faithfully, but they couldn't bear to see the child who grew up profoundly retarded. Jann's mother still kept him at her side. Never was there a question that he would become part of the *bui doi*, the "dust of life," a homeless child. Now, with the huge check from the business merger, he would always be safe, at least for whatever life he had left.

The odd thing, said Mailin, was that Howard was the center of all their lives. Everything they did, all the plans they made, were to ensure his safety. Much as she didn't like Parker, she had to give him credit for never giving up. With a mother, you expect that. Not always with a father. They never had another child, of course, for fear of possible genetic damage. Also, another child would mean less money to send home for Howard. They did everything they could, though, everything in the world that was in any way possible.

Except for the one thing they couldn't bring themselves to do. They never saw their son again.

EIGHTEEN

STRIPES OF late-afternoon sun crossed the patterned carpet from all the west windows. Mailin's story left us all sobered. Perhaps there were those in the room who could pass judgment on a couple who abandoned their only child. I, certainly, could not. He was in loving hands and besides, the LeMays were far better able to provide for him by coming to the United States. Still, the choice must have cost them a part of their humanity. We probably all wondered at that moment what we would have done.

The phone's sharp ring, when it came, jarred nerves. Morrisey answered, handed the phone to Mailin, and listened as she told the front desk she didn't know any longer when she'd be leaving. Her suitcases were still standing near the door of her room and she looked at them as if they belonged to a stranger.

Morrisey was trying to recover his professionalism. "You'd really like to go home, I know," he said, rising to his feet. "We'll wrap this up as soon as we can so you can be on your way."

Something, perhaps her being a single woman, reminded me of Hallie. I had a sudden thought. "You haven't had any unwanted visitors, by any chance, have you?"

Bingo. "You mean those men? The ones who come here?"

Morrisey had started toward the door but stopped in mid-step. "What men?"

Mailin picked up a matchbook from the table and started opening and shutting the cardboard flap. "They come yesterday. Two men, ugly men. They tell me not talk about my sister. Not to anybody. And not talk about the things she buried." She made a fist with her right hand and shook it. "They do this. Make me scared. Yes, I really, really want to go home."

I knew right away who they were. I was awed with Mailin for ignoring their warning and talking to us, since I had a pretty good idea just how ugly they could be. What kind of life had she led that she could take something so frightening in stride? Since they'd almost certainly found her through the address in my purse, I felt responsible.

Morrisey asked her to repeat anything they said, though she hadn't much to add. Then I tossed her the obvious question. "Had you ever seen those men before? Did you know who they were?"

She looked off into space, remembering. "I think I see them once. But not really sure. Maybe in car, waiting for Nicholas Qualls. One, maybe, there. He come up to the loft to talk. Qualls, I mean. They stay in car."

Munz snorted. "Qualls again." Then he looked embarrassed to have been caught talking at all. I saw Albert take both detectives aside and guessed he was telling them that our mystery woman thought her apartment had been broken into also.

Morrisey nodded, his lower lip between his teeth. "It seems we're going to have to put a little more pressure on this Qualls guy. Get him back here," he added. To Munz, "I've got a friend on the Kansas City P.D. Let's give him a call when we get back."

We all had a few more questions and asked them, but the day was winding down. Mailin knew nothing about the plane, who might have sabotaged it. She couldn't imagine that anyone would have hurt her sister. Jann crashed the plane because she was too sick to fly, and that was Parker's fault for making her go. She was totally convinced that she was right, and logic was not likely to shake her. Actually, there seemed little to be gained in forcing her to accept a murder. We left her alone in the darkening hotel room, sitting with her back to the fine views of a city she wanted desperately to leave.

Of course, the whole scene we had just witnessed might well have been a con. The bottom line was that this woman was soon to leave the country with a very large amount of money, and that sum was simply the amount we knew about. Who could determine what else she had, what the jewels, for example, were really worth. She might have arranged to have someone sabotage the plane. She might, certainly, have killed Parker, put a phony business card in his hand, and left the body to be found after she was gone. There could be a secret, unpleasant family history we could only guess at. And she was, after all, the last one to see him alive. A complicated woman, this one, and by no means short on nerve. I was grateful to Morrisey for seeing to it that she didn't yet leave town.

Albert took me back to the restaurant to pick up my rental from the parking lot. It seemed to be okay, if depressingly ugly. He followed me to the house.

The boys were home, scarfing leftover pasta primavera cold. No matter when they last ate, the very process of arriving in their own house made them ravenous. They were still high after the stress of the day, relieved that the test was over and still rehashing various questions between them. Millie had abandoned the kitchen for the weekend, having left enough possibilities for the boys to make a Saturday night meal for themselves. We, she knew, would probably go out.

We gathered around the kitchen table. Between bites of linguine, they went over the day's events. Most memorable moment: one classmate fainting from nerves. Poor kid, I thought. Forget the scores. He'd remember this day when he was eighty-five.

Both Paul and Spence were sure they'd blown every section. Afterward, they'd compared notes with Tyler Oates, who was so smart, as well as being lucky enough to be an only child, and who had none of the same answers they did. They were convinced they'd flunked completely, each of them vying for the honor of having done the worst. I'd heard it all before. They were incorrigible academic pessimists. Too much had happened today for me to get into any kind of stew about a test that was already over, though deep in my competitive soul I'd have been a little happier if Tyler's answers had jived with theirs. Ah, well. People don't have to be National Merit Finalists to live good and useful lives. We told the twins to go call Baltimore and their grandmother who was waiting to hear about the experience. Having finished off the last of the pasta as an hors d'oeuvre, they disappeared agreeably toward two of the phone extensions.

We checked Millie's messages. Albert's quartet cellist wanted to know if we'd like two tickets for tonight to a recital series. Richard Goode playing Schubert. They'd bought seats for the season, but had a conflict. The message had been left early and we figured, correctly, they'd probably found someone else for the tickets when we didn't respond. Alas. Our neighbors down the street wondered if we'd like to go out for a bite at the new Italian place that opened a mile or so away. Albert's father had called in high dudgeon about a welfare bill up before Congress of which he'd just become aware. What did Albert think? Millie, to her credit, left long and detailed messages. The one at the end was the shortest but it was the one that made Albert perk up instantly. "Your plane," it said, "has arrived."

I knew what Sunday would bring.

Even though last night we'd eaten the pasta that the boys had finished off this afternoon, and even though we'd had pizza for lunch, we called the neighbors to make reservations for the Italian place. Perhaps some hidden Neapolitan ancestors? The evening was spent talking about kids and schools and colleges and things that had nothing whatsoever to do with a violent world. No suicide, no murder, no illicit romance or illegal exports. The homemade bread was dripping with oil and covered with large chunks of fresh garlic. Heaven. Later, we had to find a way to be together without breathing on each other. Tricky, but not impossible.

The next morning, after Sunday funnies, the *Times* crossword, and a breakfast created by all of us amateurs, the boys took off for a scheduled game of touch football and Albert went to get his flight bag. We stopped by Millie's closed door and told her we'd be back later. She grunted. She always grunts on Sunday.

The Aurora was promised for tomorrow. There was no way I was setting foot inside that rental, so we fired up Albert's rough-riding four-wheel-drive and headed for the airport. I was resigned. We weren't really planning to go anywhere and that was a plus. Today, it was just a question of greeting the new plane, *Sweet Juliet*'s successor, and taking it up for a preliminary spin. I couldn't be so cruel as not to share such an important moment with Albert. The arrival of a new plane isn't quite comparable to a conversion experience, but it's only an electron ring or so behind. If it stayed as fine a day as it was now, Albert assured me, maybe we'd fly a little further but we wouldn't be in the air for more than an hour or so. That was the plan. What is it about plans?

NINETEEN

I SUPPOSE what happened that day could be laid rather directly on me. Heading back to the funny road in the mountains, the one we suspected was serving as an impromptu landing strip, was my idea. Since I was going to endure another session in the probably turbulent skies, and in a different, untested plane, the least Albert could do was go where I wanted. Somewhere teasing my imagination was the thought that maybe we should try landing there after all and going to look for a hidden stash of who knew what radioactive material. Of course, I didn't tell Albert anything like that. Besides, we didn't happen to have a Geiger counter or scintillometer. Still, I had the feeling tracks or footprints or something would lead us to the spot. Well, hey, anything's possible.

Jack Potts emerged from the hangar, wiping his hands on a paper towel. I should have known he'd be here. The man never stayed in his house if he could help it. The new-to-us Turbo Arrow had been repainted, washed, and waxed. It glistened like a piece of Czech crystal. Tony, Albert's former flying instructor, saw us and came over to add his admiration. Sally from the FBO desk waved from a distance and made a circle with her thumb and forefinger. Everyone loves the luster of new toys.

Albert was completely thrilled. The last time I'd seen an expression of such bliss on his face, he'd held his twins for the first time. With Potts, he walked all around this new baby, peering in at the luggage area, lifting the cowling, caressing the center point of the propeller, touching everything. I patted the fuselage without enthusiasm. To me, it looked a lot like *Sweet Juliet* only nicer, newer. I hoped it had a better prognosis.

Potts had, of course, gone over everything with meticulous care. The preflight and run-up went without incident and, once the tower gave the clearance, we were aloft in moments, banking high around the airport and heading generally north. That's when I tendered my suggestion about the mountain road.

"You actually *want* to fly into the mountains?"

We both wore voice-activated headsets, making our speech sound like an alien pilot from a Close Encounter. "Actually, no. But it might be interesting to see the road again. Now that Parker's dead, there may be no one else still living, besides us, that is, who's aware of the place. And who knows what got left behind? There could be something in the truck, or maybe a path to the hiding place."

Albert, who normally kept an alert eye on both the horizon and the instruments, broke away to look at me, amazed. "Are you actually suggesting that we *land* there? Am I really hearing this from you?"

I smiled nervously. "Maybe. And maybe I'll fink out once we get there and I remember how high those mountains are. But why not at least aim in that direction?"

"Sure. No problem." I think he was grinning.

He banked the plane again, this time sharply to the left, and the compass needle swung to "W." The foothills rose in front of us, and behind them the high peaks, now covered heavily with early snow. Albert added power and lifted the nose till the new plane could reach an acceptable altitude for a mountain flight. "Feel this baby climb," he exulted. "It's more responsive than the old one by half. Grand, ain't it?" This was one happy man. I felt my stomach stay a thousand feet behind.

Albert hadn't plotted a route for this detour. In fact, he hadn't planned a trip, but we were actually not all that far from home base. Charts for the area were in his case, but he didn't seem to need them. He did mutter something about not bothering to file a flight plan. Mountain flying took all his concentration. I could feel the pull of erratic wind patterns as we passed over uneven ground and began to regret my curiosity. He'd radio our location once we landed, *if* we landed. As for direction, his instincts took over, along with the memory of the last time we were there. I vaguely recognized certain distinctive craggy hills and passes as we neared what I remembered to be that unexpected high plateau. The plane crested a ridge of moderate peaks and, as before, we were suddenly there, staring at the abandoned road.

It had been a great idea. The only problem was, we weren't the first people to have it.

I didn't recognize the plane that sat facing the

abrupt drop-off where the road ended. It was a low-wing single engine, but bigger and sleeker than anything we'd ever flown. Something about it looked mega-powerful, a leopard ready to spring. We could see a hint of motion through the front window, perhaps the pilot still making adjustments. Maybe the group had just arrived. On the ground, two men looked up when they heard our engine. One was wearing a green jacket. My hand reached out for Albert's arm. "Qualls's men," I said. "I'm almost sure. That looks like the Tornado."

Whatever they'd been planning to do at that moment apparently changed when they saw us. We could almost imagine the voices, the quick consultations, the shouted orders. They began running toward the plane, grabbing several small bags from the ground, throwing them through the door, and then jumping in themselves.

"That's a Mirage," said Albert, too surprised by the machine to sense the danger I was feeling. "A plane our friend Qualls might like a lot. Very big bucks. Think the new ones are upwards of seven hundred thousand dollars. Made by Piper, too, but trust me, we're just poor relations." He banked again to take another fly-by. "Whoever landed it on that road is some kind of pilot."

Nervous as I was at this unexpected encounter, I knew what it meant. We weren't the only living people who knew, or suspected, the secret of the radioactive drop. Qualls himself must have been told. Probably that's what he'd bought when he decided to go for the "merger." I wondered if Parker had taken him here, shown him the stash to prove its worth. Once Qualls knew, of course, he didn't need its owner anymore. The day Parker took his new "partner" to see this utilitarian closed road, he may have written his own obituary.

We were too high to see faces, but I had a very good mental image of one or two. Though the interior of the plane was cool, its air vents open, I could feel a rash of sweat drops break out on my forehead. "Okay, stop playing around and let's get out of here. I'm sorry I ever suggested this, big time. They're obviously very agitated to have been seen here. In a minute, they're going to decide to come after us."

I guess they heard me. Psychically. Once they had all piled into the plane and secured the door, we could see the propeller start to rotate. Albert made one more quick banking turn to be sure and then swung back the way we'd come. "You may be right. They might just be leaving. Flying home after a little outing. But why don't I believe that?" The new plane, not yet comfortable in Albert's hands, shuddered slightly at the abrupt change in direction and then, at its pilot's touch on the throttle, picked up speed. On the ground, just before we lost sight of the road behind mountains, we saw the Mirage do a tight one-eighty and start its takeoff.

Turbulence in planes gets worse when the speed is increased. I could feel the air become much less stable than it had been before and it's never completely stable in the mountains, anyway. I found myself grabbing the door strap with one hand and the back of Albert's seat with the other, my usual death grip. The plane hit an air pocket, dropped a hundred fast feet, and recovered. I breathed deeply and tried to quiet my traumatized stomach. "Can they catch us?" I asked shakily.

"In a heartbeat. But what can they do then? They can hardly ram us without hurting their own plane. This isn't the Los Angeles freeway. They can't force us off the road."

The plane was beginning to shake. I wondered how fast one had to go before the whole thing fell apart. Ahead of us, the high mountains of the mid-Rockies towered majestically. A few thick white clouds, the kind shaped like cotton candy on a cone of paper, had formed at our backs. They weren't, I realized, as sweet. "Storm clouds?" I asked, afraid of the answer.

"I don't think so. But don't worry, we can avoid them. We're really not that far from the airport. Twenty minutes, maybe, if we could fly a straight line."

"Albert, those really are Qualls's men. I'm sure of it."

"From this altitude?"

"Yes, really. And they're coming after us."

"What, a friendly group like that? Do you see them anywhere?"

I twisted in my seat, finally unlatching the seat belt, so I could see what, if anything, was coming from behind. Oh, for a rear window. The plane was a mass of blind spots. Nothing appeared on my side.

I swung as far as possible the other way to check Albert's side and the backseat windows. My heart sank. "No, no, no, no, no. They're here. We have company."

Albert swiveled to look over his shoulder and the plane bucked, making him turn back fast. "Okay, so they're tailing us. I told you, there's nothing they can do. They'll probably just follow us back to the airport and have some kind of confrontation." He looked at me to make sure I hadn't completely self-destructed. "We're okay. We'll be fine."

I glanced out to see if we'd somehow managed to lose the "traffic," and literally couldn't believe my eyes. I blinked and tried to refocus. The plane was dangerously close to us now, crazily close, so close I could read most of the numbers. In all my limited experience, I'd never seen a plane buzz another this way. Madness. A large gun barrel, bigger than most of the handguns I'd seen in movies, had emerged from the pilot's storm window, the flap most fliers used simply to shout "Clear!" No face was visible, but I could see the hand. It was curled around the butt and the trigger.

My first instinct was to laugh. A gun, sticking out of a rich man's toy, a plane that was meant to fly to Las Vegas for the weekend or Dallas for a meeting. Ridiculous. It was a plaything, not a fighter; a poodle, not a Doberman. But there was that terrible gun, and I couldn't wish it away.

Instead I screamed.

The Mirage pulled up to a spot maybe fifty feet above us on Albert's side where I had only too clear a view and I watched with horror as the shaking barrel pointed at us. A bullet grazed the front window, leaving behind an arced trail of etched Plexiglas. I smelled a wave of my own sweat. Even with earphones, I could hear the screech. At least it hadn't hit either of us. Albert, stricken, looked at the track in disbelief, a terrible scar on what had been his perfect, almost-new plane. Then he howled, outraged. "Those bloody idiots! What do they think they're doing, playing war games?" He tightened his grip on the yoke. "Okay, they want war, they've got war." The plane jumped, returned.

I waited for the nausea that was never far behind when I flew, but it didn't come. Raw fear works great on motion sickness. We bucked and dove, banked and circled, providing a close-to-impossible target for the enemy. When I could catch sight of the Mirage, the gunman seemed not to be aiming, as if waiting for us to wear out from the exhausting aerobatics. Albert was drum-tight, checking the altimeter, checking the horizon, adjusting the throttle, and now and then the mixture, but most of all, working the yoke. Ahead of us and coming quickly closer were the clouds we'd seen earlier, now starting to form a thick bank.

"They have their window open, right?"

I looked again to be sure. The Mirage had drifted above us again and to the right, but I could see the gun barrel still in position through the pilot's flap. "Yes. Why?"

"Because that's a pressurized plane. Or is when

the window isn't open. It's not pressurized now. Do you see our oxygen tank behind you on the floor?''

I twisted around again. "Yes. Shall I get it?"

"Wait a minute."

Suddenly everything around us went white as Albert flew directly into the cloud bank. "Okay," he said. "Here goes. Let's hope there's no other plane frolicking around in here."

We'd flown in clouds before, but experience didn't make it less of a disorienting act. All direction, all visual information, was gone. Instinct was totally unreliable. Albert's eyes were glued to the instruments. "Okay, get the tank. And get the oxygen going if you can while they can't see what we're doing."

By some miracle, I managed to wrestle the heavy thing up from the backseat and into my lap. As often as we'd flown, I'd never had to use the tank. The nose cannulas were wrapped around the top. I separated them, twisted the obvious knob, and handed one of the plastic tubes to Albert. I couldn't hear a hiss, had no idea if oxygen was coming through or not. He let go of the yoke long enough to fasten the oxygen to his nose, telling me to do the same. It felt invasive. In a split second, I forgot it was there. "Now," he said, "we're going up."

He turned east, emerging from the cloud bank into clear sunlight. Beautiful, clear sunlight. I wanted to believe he really knew that the clouds ended there, that he hadn't just got lucky. We could see again, a definite plus for a pilot who hadn't yet earned his instrument rating. The Mirage wasn't in sight.

Maybe they'd followed us into the cumulus bank. He pulled back on the yoke and I watched as the altimeter needle started to creep up above fourteen thousand feet. Once more, I started to panic.

"What are you doing? This isn't a DC-10."

The needle read 15,500 and was still climbing. "Pressurized planes get a little lax about auxiliary oxygen, and I'm willing to bet they're not even thinking about the fact that they lost their pressure when they decided to open their window and shoot at us. I suppose it's possible somebody thought to use the dump valve before they took off. That way they were never pressurized, so there was no moment when it was suddenly lost. But I'll bet they're so used to ignoring cabin pressure, they won't even think about it. And my guess is they're going to feel this."

His mouth tightened as the plane climbed to seventeen thousand feet.

"How high are we going?"

"We can get to twenty thousand on a good day. And this looks like a good day."

"Oh, no." I buried my head in a hand, closing my eyes so I couldn't see the needle go round. "They won't kill us. You will."

"We're not going to stay up here long. Just long enough to muddle their little sea-level brain cells, assuming you're right that they're Qualls's men."

I'd managed to rebuckle my seat belt, though it seemed a little irrational to think it could save my life after a drop from twenty thousand feet. Stupidly, it struck me as really unfair that Albert should die in a plane he hadn't yet had a chance to fall in love with. Nothing was making any kind of sense. "Can we call somebody?" I asked. "Tell them what's happening? I caught most of the numbers on the plane. Maybe if they know the tower is aware…"

At that moment, I saw the Mirage. They saw us, too, and fired erratically in our direction. Albert banked abruptly away from the flash. "Yes, call," he said tensely. "I don't think I can keep this up. I'm going to try to head back to the airport. Call the tower. Call emergency."

"What, me? I've never used the radio!"

"Well, sweetheart, I'd do it for you but I'm just a little too busy right now." He banked again in the opposite direction, swinging the plane around and under the line of fire.

I could see the microphone. That part was obvious. To talk, you pushed down on the little gizmo. But the dials, the buttons, the readouts! All those frequencies, and only one of them would get the tower. I'd spent the time since Albert learned to fly resolutely resisting any knowledge of how these things worked. If he'd had a heart attack and died while touring us around, I'd just decided to die with him. Life wouldn't be any fun without him anyway, so why work to save something that had lost all value? The twins were a problem, of course. I owed it to them to hang around till they were self-sustaining, but they were closing in. They'd be fine.

That was in normal times. But now I was mad. Really mad. Someone had to be told what was going on so that even if they succeeded in shooting us down, no one would ever be able to say that pilot error was at fault. Somehow, that would be unbearable. *So…think.*

If my memory for numbers was ever going to prove itself out, this was the time. The dial in my head turned up 7700. What was it? Squawk. Squawk 7700 for emergencies. On the transponder. That was the readout right in front of me. I turned the knob one way and then the other till the 7700 came up. The light kept flashing. Had I really done anything? I looked at Albert, thought about asking him, and decided against it. He was rigid, tense, completely in the zone. Now what? I had no idea what the tower frequency was. It changed every time we came to a different airport. Granted, it would have been nice to know the one for our *own* airport, but I didn't. So be it. 121.5. What was that? Numbers Albert told me to remember. All right, 121.5 it is. Maybe that reached Afghanistan, but I had nothing else to try. I fooled with the dials on the radio till the numbers came up someplace. Then it was a question of punching another knob, bouncing that magic number left and right and then back again. I settled for left. I picked up the mike, pushed the button, and shouted at it, "Help. SOS. Mayday, Mayday. There's a plane here that's trying to kill us."

Albert glanced fast at me, his expression unreadable. A voice in my ear asked who I was.

I started to give the usual numbers and then realized they belonged to *Sweet Juliet*. I had no idea what the new plane's numerical name was. "I'm sorry. This is Grace Beckmann. My husband, Albert

Beckmann, is flying the plane. But I don't know what it's called." My eyes caught an N number on a piece of tape above the instruments. "Wait, I have it." I read it off. "Okay? Now. Nicholas Qualls is shooting at us from a Mirage. Call Detective Morrisey at the police department." I gave the number. "Tell him to get to the airport."

"Did you say shooting?"

"Yes. Shooting. From a Mirage, number..." I reeled them off. "Does that help?"

"That is affirmative. We will clear the field for an emergency landing."

"Thank you."

He encouraged me to keep in contact. I had to marvel at how serene and composed the man at the other end of my transmission managed to sound. I'd just told him an idiotic story, a wildly improbable tale, and he responded as if I'd asked for a weather briefing. I thanked him again, replaced the microphone in its holder, and looked over at Albert.

He turned to me with a little smile. "Let's hope our friends in the Mirage heard that. It would help a lot if they knew their cover was blown. With luck, they won't dare shoot at us now. And incidentally..." He gave my knee a smart slap. "You were great. And you remembered the emergency frequency."

Emergency frequency? So it wasn't Afghanistan.

We were out of the mountains now and on a steep descent to a landing altitude. I had no idea how long we'd been racing away from the enemy, but it felt like hours. I checked my watch. We'd been ap-

proaching the hidden road only about thirty minutes
earlier. Now the vast plains were visible to the east,
a darker purple as they receded to the horizon. The
Mirage was nowhere to be seen. I spotted the runway in the distance and, thanks to my radio pal,
there were no planes anywhere near it. Our own airport always looked good to me, but never had it
been more beautiful. The Taj Mahal by moonlight
couldn't hold a candle.

Relief flooded over me, along with an enormous
appreciation for Albert's skill. No pro could have
done it any better. With the relief, however, came
another more demanding sensation. I leaned over
and dumped everything out of my purse onto the
cabin floor. Then, using the empty bag in a way for
which it was never intended, I discreetly threw up
Sunday brunch.

My last good purse had been stolen. This life was
hard on purses.

TWENTY

MORRISEY WAS waiting for us in the area where the tower had instructed us to taxi in. The man had moved fast, and on a Sunday, too. At that moment, I would have given to any charity that claimed to represent the police department, phony or not.

The sharp sunlight cast hard shadows on his face, deepening the lines of concern. His worry was obvious in the frown and the tension of his grip on a black carrying case. Once we deplaned and walked toward him, looking, amazingly, only fractionally the worse for wear, he relaxed. "Nice landing," he said with a wry smile.

"Didn't exactly grease it." Albert sighed. "But under the circumstances…"

"Right." The detective was a little abstracted. He watched me walk to the nearest trash bin and drop my purse through the hole.

I saw his look. "Don't ask," I said.

Albert was talking to some men near the plane, pointing out the scar on the windshield and joining them as they checked out the Arrow for further damage. I didn't know who they were, and I didn't know who was with Morrisey. Munz wasn't there. Instead, several others who might have been detectives, plus two uniformed policemen, were nearby. I went into the nearby FBO's bathroom to calm my still-shaking hands under very warm water. The face I saw in the mirror was the color of slightly moldy Camembert. Blusher would have helped, but I'd left it on the floor of the plane.

By the time I emerged, a small crowd had gathered around Albert and Morrisey. No one seemed inclined to let me push my way in, so I listened from the periphery. Apparently, I gathered from the people nearest me, a Malibu Mirage had radioed a request for an emergency landing. Well, well. Obviously a big morning for emergency landings. Now, how many Mirages did I imagine could be out flying right here and now?

I yelled to make myself heard over the people and general airport noise. "Did they say what kind of emergency?"

Morrisey saw me then and motioned for the crowd to let me through. "Something about a major gas leak. Do you think the shooter might have put a bullet through his own plane?"

"She's the one to ask," said Albert with a hint of pride. "I had all I could do to stay in the air. Grace handled the radio and kept her eye on the Mirage."

Bloody amazing. I have sold long pieces to major magazines, given birth to twins and gone home in two days, entertained at wonderfully gemutlich dinner parties peopled with the best and brightest and brought a dying giant ficus back to life, all winning gratitude but not much in the way of praise. But yell "Mayday" into a hand microphone and watch in horror while crazy people are shooting at us through a tiny storm window flap and I'm a heroine. You don't always know what move is going to win the game.

I went for an aw-shucks-it-was-nothing attitude. "Sure they could have put a bullet into their own plane accidentally. It was turbulent, we were all going fast. All I saw was the hand of the man holding the gun, but it was shaking. He might have caught his own wing."

"With the gas tank."

The crowd was growing and the press had somehow picked up on the situation, probably hearing the exchange with a radio tuned to the tower. Sundays being slow news days, a nice little drama like this could be a godsend for the five o'clock lead. Everyone was scanning the sky.

I wondered why they hadn't tried to turn back, leave the state, do anything rather than land at the precise airport where we, their would-be victims, had certainly headed. Only an extreme emergency would have forced them down here. They must really have been too short of gas to make it anywhere else. Had they flown in from Kansas City? That would make a dent in their supply. Then, with a bullet through one tank...

We heard the drone of the plane, then, at a distance, we saw it crest the foothills. It seemed to be wobbling, its wings losing and finding the horizontal, but it might simply have been a factor of the wind which had picked up substantially.

Despite the rocky approach, the Mirage landed without incident. The police had all hit their cars before the landing. Brakes squealed as some of the black-and-whites skidded sideways, then followed the plane right down the runway. Others attempted to intercept and head it off from nearby taxiways. The plane shimmied and came to a stop. By the time the propeller stopped turning and the door opened, half a dozen members of the force had drawn their guns and aimed. They surrounded the Mirage.

One of the passengers appeared at the plane's door and looked around, seemingly a bit dazed. His muscles flexed, tightening his stance. Then his shoulders sagged. He jumped down, raised his hands, and gave up.

Two more men and the pilot appeared, expressionless. I didn't recognize the first man. The pilot looked familiar. It occurred to me that he might be the one we'd seen with the corporate jet earlier in the week. The other two, however, had performed a grotesque dance through my dreams for many days: Nicholas Qualls and the Tornado. Beautiful. A clean sweep.

Everyone around us started running toward the action, the ones with cameras moving fastest. Morrisey restrained us from following, grasping our arms with his powerful hands. "They'll be taken to the station where we can talk to them," he said quietly. "Leave your car here and come with me. I'll have someone drive you back later to pick it up."

Albert gave me a once-over. "You okay?"

"Yeah."

"Not nauseated?"

"My legs still think they're flying, but the stomach recognizes land. I'm fine."

He turned to Morrisey. "We can drive. We'll meet you at the station within the hour."

"That'll be fine."

Then, after watching Morrisey leave and checking again to see that I wasn't in danger of an immediate breakdown, Albert headed out to the field to deal with the plane and I went back into the FBO. Empty of loiterers, most of whom had probably wandered out on the field, the lobby looked serene in the light from large picture windows. The always-running TV, just as I turned toward it, interrupted their regular programming to announce double emergency landings at the city's general aviation airport. I watched as if the whole thing had happened to someone else. Fast work, that bulletin. Impressive. Nothing I'd ever done in the journalism field had such a degree of immediacy. I envied it.

By the time we arrived at the station, the story had been running on all the radio and TV channels, picking up details as it went along. Our names, though not the names of the passengers in the other plane, were announced on the fifty-thousand-watt station. We'd have a hundred messages from colleagues far and near once we got home.

Morrisey came out to the lobby. He sat on an institutional chair at right angles to our couch, hands on his knees. "There's something I've been meaning to tell you for the last couple of days, but things have been happening too fast."

We waited while he worked out his approach to the story.

"The lawyer, your Mr. Westgaard, was located by some friends of ours in Costa Rica. They had a long talk."

"Did he do the plane? Cut it? Was he out to get me?" Albert was stoic.

"No, no. It hadn't anything to do with you directly. But he was involved in his own way." Morrisey closed his eyes against a sudden ray of sun coming through a distant window. "He saw Jann LeMay about a week before she died and realized something was wrong. She looked, he said, like someone in the last stages of cancer. He figured, knowing how close she and Parker were, that Parker wouldn't be able to go on without her and that his deal was about to go kaput. Without the buyout or merger, whatever, to put immediate money in his pocket, he'd go to jail for fraud. So he split."

"Are you planning to extradite him? Can you?"

"He's coming back on his own. The Qualls deal will make him well after all...assuming it still goes through. Big assumption at this point. Of course, he's still guilty of theft, fraud, a few other things, but replacing the money will help a lot."

"And what are the chances, after this morning, that Qualls can go through with whatever it is?" I asked.

Morrisey stood, straightening his sleeves. "Let's go find out."

I was sorry to leave the large, quiet lobby, so different, I was sure, from what awaited us upstairs.

We walked up a flight, down a long, narrow hall and into an area the size of a third-grade classroom. I was right. Voices coming from open doors along the way were tense and angry. In the room, clutter made the walls shrink inward. Locked filing cabinets lined the periphery, extra chairs were stacked in one corner and six or seven unopened cardboard boxes piled up almost to the ceiling. In the center, under a fluorescent light, was a large gray metal table and four or five chairs. It would have looked right at home in a TV cop show.

"This isn't our regular interrogation room. It's bigger. I wanted space for you to sit in," said the detective, pulling out a chair for me. "Not quite orthodox, but you've been part of this affair since the beginning and in fact I very much doubt if we'd be at this stage without you." He began to pace. "We're bringing in Qualls, and I want him to see you sitting here. Let's say it might help him cut the... Well, you know." He found a toothpick in his pants pocket and fingered it thoughtfully. "If anyone still alive knows the story, it's him. We just have to convince him to tell it to us."

The chair was uncompromising. I pushed mine a little further back from the table in a not so subtle attempt to distance myself from what was going to happen. If I could have done it without notice, I'd have scooted into one corner, losing myself in the shadow. I hadn't bargained for this. Qualls scared me but it was more than that.

Why did I feel that a man who, in all likelihood, had killed two people, and certainly tried to kill us, should be treated differently? What was bothering me about this scene?

He entered the room, accompanied and hand-cuffed, and scanned the area with a look that dismissed the surroundings. His cuffs were removed once he was seated and he rubbed his wrists thoughtfully. Albert and I bothered his conscience not at all. So much for Morrisey's Plan A. His eyes passed over us with the same cool disdain that he used to note the tin ashtray on the ledge.

My compassion was gone in a heartbeat. I was furious. "Gee," I said. "We survived. And here you did your best to kill us. What a loser."

He didn't even look up. "Just trying to scare you." That was obviously going to be his eventual defense.

He and Morrisey started talking about what each wanted and what each would bring to the table in exchange. Anyone else would have waited for a lawyer. Qualls was obviously the kind of guy who figured he could handle everything himself. Morrisey was offering some major concessions, or anyway seemed to be, in exchange for the total story. I tuned the details out. All I wanted was to know what had happened. If he killed Jann and Parker, he'd say so when the time came and say it with a certain arrogance. He wasn't the type to grovel. He was the type to lie but he could hardly deny what had happened this morning. Not, in any case, with us sitting here. Finally, the detective began asking the questions I was waiting for.

"You understand," he said to Qualls, "that we'll

check everything you say and if it looks like you're not leveling, all deals are off.''

Qualls leaned against the table, fixing Morrisey with eyes that peered from half-lowered lids. "Go ahead.'' He hadn't belonged with the group of "nice" people at Jann's memorial service, and he didn't belong here. This was a man who would never fit in no matter where he was and who not only realized the fact but relished it.

"All right. When the Beckmanns spotted your plane earlier today at the mountain landing strip, were you planning to look for a hidden cache of radioactive material?''

Qualls studied the tips of his fingers, bringing them together tentlike on the table. He was surely unused to speaking openly about his business matters, criminal or otherwise, for any number of reasons. For a minute, I thought his natural reticence would win out and he'd refuse to answer after all, but he surprised me. Once the words started, they came easily.

"No need to look. I knew where it was. We were going to make a withdrawal. We were prepared to take it back with us.''

"How did you know where to find it?''

"Parker took me there once. And Jann did, too.''

"Were you going to steal it?''

Qualls sat back, offended. "Of course not. I paid for that stuff, that and the contacts for more. A million bucks. Our deal was no 'merger,' no matter what he said. It was a simple buyout. His company wasn't worth a cent without the cesium. That and a few other...commodities.''

"Then what would Parker do?" Albert apparently still felt something for his old partner.

"He would have waited a reasonable length of time and folded up shop. All that ever mattered was the money, the upfront money. He didn't have a long view, not that guy. Whatever Parker LeMay was or was not, he was never a businessman. Without his wife, he'd have gone under long ago. Almost did, in fact.''

Morrisey stared at him thoughtfully. He waited a long moment and then said, "Once you knew those contacts and where they kept their stock, you didn't need them any more, did you." It wasn't a question.

Qualls chose to ignore the implications. "They showed me everything," he agreed. "Told me what kind of plane was needed to land on the mountain road. Warned me about handling the stuff. Apparently, they thought one of their young workers was killed by accidental radiation exposure, though the fact wasn't picked up. That was one of the reasons they said they wanted out. That and the money.''

Trisha Potts, I thought. Did her death start the progression that ended in all this tragedy? And what was that about a million dollars? What happened to the rest of the money? Mailin had claimed she received only half that. Half the payout was missing. Was she lying?

"They operated in good faith," Qualls continued. "It was going to be pretty clean.''

A uniformed policewoman chose that moment to

enter the room with a message for the detective, one she delivered quietly into his ear. She had a gently rounded figure and somewhat serious demeanor that seemed to clash slightly with the pleasant face. The message delivered, she handed Morrisey a sheaf of papers, exposing an angry red mark on one arm.

"What happened here, Maureen?" he asked, taking the offending limb gently in his hand.

She withdrew the arm, embarrassed, rubbing the redness lightly. The mark was about three inches long and an inch wide. The area looked painful, cracked, and sore. "Oh, it was just dumb," she said. "I burned it on the top of the oven taking out a twenty-pound turkey. From now on, I get my husband to lift those suckers."

A burn. Images started flying like the electronic missiles on the boys' computer games. I could immediately reconstruct pictures from the articles in the library that awful day, photos of the survivors of nuclear disasters. Radiation burns. The sheriff's men talking about the mark on Jann's leg. A burn? Oh, great, how had I missed this for so long?

I emerged from my startled thoughts just in time to hear Morrisey hit Qualls with the critical question, the one he'd been holding in reserve. "Then why did you kill them?"

I saved them both the trouble of a denial. "He didn't," I said.

Qualls sat back, folding his arms across his chest. He found the only window in the room with his eyes and looked out at the square foot of sky as if someone up there were telling a joke only he could hear. "She's right. I didn't."

Morrisey looked from Qualls to me and then back again, thrown off stride. "Are you saying you didn't kill Jann?"

"Ask her. She knows the answers." He stared at me, knowing what it would do to me to have to answer.

Morrisey obligingly turned to me. "Well?"

"He didn't. He didn't kill her."

"What about Parker? Did he kill him?"

"No."

"Then who did?"

"Parker did," I said.

Albert broke the silence first. "Gracie, what are you talking about?"

I nodded at Qualls, knowing this was his moment. "Let him tell you."

A smile of sorts softened the handsome, menacing face. "She's right again, the little lady," said the man who had recently wanted me dead. "The occasionally amazing Parker LeMay killed his wife and he killed himself, though he did make an attempt to have it look like I had done it. But he was bitter by the end and not operating that well. Everything was gone. I guess he wanted to believe the fault was mine and tried to take me with him."

I pointed an accusing finger, leaning toward him angrily. "And probably the fault was yours," I said. "Did you pressure them? Make them take chances, skip precautions to meet some kind of deadline?" I sat back again, shaking my head. "I'll bet you did."

His defenses returned. "They knew the risks," he said, his voice pure ice. "I was in a hurry."

"Westgaard probably turned on the pressure, too," added Albert. "That fight in the airport. Telling Parker that Jann looked like she was dying."

"Go on," said Morrisey. "What happened?"

Qualls studied a bit of chipped paint on the table, flicking it with a fingernail. "Parker told me the whole story a few days before he died, about the boy they left behind, about how the sister found the cesium contact and how Jann's relationship with the governor made it all possible. Nice, wasn't it? I wouldn't mind having a woman like that at my side."

"The irony," I interrupted, "is that those two people loved each other to the exclusion, practically, of the rest of the world." I could feel the blood come to my face. "In fact, I'm still having trouble with this, even knowing it's probably true. You must have forced him to do the murder."

Qualls observed my agitation with an irritating lack of concern. "Mrs. Beckmann, hasn't it occurred to you yet that you're missing something? We Greeks understand the concept of the tragic flaw in people otherwise quite admirable. When the LeMays left their son behind, that was the seed, the 'flaw.' The flower, if you will, was their death. You see, Jann spent a great deal of time dealing with the cesium. She had to bring it over. She flew with it in your old plane many times in the course of burying and retrieving it. At some point, a bit of it must have escaped its protective shield. It lodged somewhere near her, maybe in a piece of clothing that she wore often. Parker said there were burns on her legs almost certainly caused by radiation.''

''That's how I knew just now that he'd done it.''

''Exactly. Parker knew she was going to die. She didn't. Or maybe she did and was in some kind of denial. She hadn't yet seen a doctor. In any case, he couldn't let her die a natural death, if you want to call such a death 'natural.' Someone would be sure to ask the right questions.''

''Didn't she wonder what was on her leg?''

''She knew what it was, at least according to Parker. Just didn't realize its implications.''

I'd taken the questioning away from Morrisey, but he didn't seem to mind. ''So he jimmied the plane?'' Then I answered that myself, thinking out loud. ''Why not? He was perfectly capable of it. He'd flown during the war. Knew all about planes. And, while her last moments would be very frightening, he knew the death she faced would be much much kinder in the long run than allowing the sickness to take its course. That was it, wasn't it.''

Qualls picked up the narrative. ''According to LeMay, she was failing fast. He was afraid to wait till the plane was free to send her on that last trip. Gave her some pretext to get her to 'steal' the plane from you that day and just to go. Probably told her he needed supplies right away. He knew what time you usually arrived at the hangar, so it was no problem to get her there ahead of you.''

The words were coming in a torrent now, propelled, it seemed, by the relief of confession. ''The departure that made the tower so angry, though, wasn't his idea. He said he guessed she was just in a hurry to get the job over with, this last pickup. She'd left with the empty pig. I insisted on one more sample to check before the business was turned over to me." He stretched his arms high over his head, hands interlocked, before going on. "Actually, the whole thing might have worked fine if the plane had burned. It was supposed to explode, but she was too good a pilot. If the cut cables hadn't been found, the whole operation would have been very slick.

"One other thing. I think he really did want the best for her under the circumstances, though you Puritans probably don't believe that."

I leaned back in the painfully straight chair, my mind no longer in the cheerless station. I was over the mountains again, sensing the difficult currents of air, seeing clouds and the impossibly broken land beneath. All I could think of was Jann LeMay, feeling the plane coming apart under her and knowing, almost certainly knowing, what her own trusted Parker had done to her. Did she try to tell him that she forgave him? Did she, at the last, understand? Could anyone?

And the boy, now a man, half a world away who, unaware, caused everything. Mailin, I hoped, would take his share of the money back and see to it that he lived out his life in some degree of comfort. He was the center, the whole purpose, of his parents' life, the ultimate cause of their death, but for all practical purposes he never saw them, never felt their touch or kiss. What had Qualls said about a tragic flaw? Leaving their child behind had been, perhaps, a selfish act but surely not one that deserved so terrible a punishment. A darkness seemed to come over the room.

The questioning had gone on without me. Qualls had acknowledged his plans for the use and importation of illegal radioactive drugs. He admitted setting his "assistant" to intimidate me, to stop my snooping, though the attack in the library had gotten out of hand. Apparently, he'd also admitted that, in the panic of being discovered, he'd issued the order to shoot at us. Morrisey was back in control and Albert was involved but I had, in my heart, left the place. One enormous question almost paralyzed me. Obviously, I'd had nothing to do with Parker's initial choice. He murdered his wife on his own terms. But his suicide... Did I provoke that by coming too close, by allowing him to realize that Albert and I would eventually have pried out the story?

I stood, walking over to the small window and a larger world. I'd wanted to solve the murder, and the murder was solved. My need for adventure, the fallout from my lost childhood, was probably *my* fatal flaw, but I'd lived with it most of my life and I'd deal with it now. No one makes it all the way through without molding ankle chains of twenty-four-karat guilt.

I caught Albert's eye and gestured toward the door. He was still listening to Morrisey's questioning, but aware I was becoming uncomfortable. *Let's get out of here,* I telegraphed. *Time to go home.*

SOMEDAY, I'LL WRITE UP this whole tragic story and find a market for it. Months have passed since that day we spent dodging bullets in the air, since we learned the story of the LeMays' life. For some writers, such a long period of time would have created enough distance but I think it will take me longer.

Or maybe I should forget the writing. Just let the word out that I'm available for a little discreet investigation now and then. Who ever said one shouldn't send life out on a few surprising turns?

For now, though, I have other things to do. I've finished the Native American piece for my liberal magazine, and am deeply into the planning of the family's sabbatical trip, organizing shots, everyone's clothes, my assignments. The twins' school, thanks to Colin Beardsley and maybe to our generous contributions, has been very understanding. And speaking of that, Paul turned out to be right. Spence ended up a National Merit Semifinalist. Apparently his blackjack game brought him luck. Paul didn't miss by much and, believe it or not, was genuinely happy for his brother and not at all jealous. Of course, Paul is now my special project since he will obviously need extra mothering.

Qualls is currently out on bail and working with his team of high-profile lawyers. I found I couldn't really hate him, though I'd often consigned his henchman to rot. Mailin has written to us from home, which really surprised me. She's happy to be back, and I suspect the money makes that happiness significantly sweeter. I doubt that she'll ever know the real story. Jack Potts received a totally unex-

pected check for the missing half million dollars. It
was sent by a secretary at Parker's company who
said LeMay had left instructions to do so, in memory
of Trisha.

The governor has announced, not surprisingly,
that he won't run for another term. Magda says his
wife—now that her secret is out—is reported to be
looking at houses, the more dramatic the better. I
doubt that anyone will ever be able to keep her under wraps again.

My mother isn't happy about our going so far
away, particularly into an area of the world where
the diseases are "interesting," but she's planning to
talk to Millie every day at the same time she's used
to talking to me and says she'll make do.

And Millie? She's looking forward to six months
of "Seinfeld" reruns and bratwurst eaten on paper
plates. Once we're safely gone, she's decided, every
day will be Sunday.

Albert is putting his plane into Jack Potts's hands
for the duration, but leaving it will still be unendur-
able, particularly after its sterling performance that
day in the mountains. He loves it, this high-
maintenance mistress of his. In fact, when it comes
to the plane, I worry sometimes that he's losing it.
Yesterday, I actually saw him kiss its cowling.

killing thyme

PETER ABRESCH

A JAMES P. DANDY ELDERHOSTEL MYSTERY

Take a few ambitious chefs, a handful of amateur cooks on a week-long tour of Baltimore's greatest restaurants, season with a bit of competition for a spot on a new TV show, "A Dash of Thyme," throw in a ruthless killer and voilà, a perfectly seasoned dish of homicide.

Amateur sleuths James P. Dandy and his ladylove Dodee Swisher embark on a culinary caper as delicious as it is deadly—with a clever killer who's eager to serve them just desserts.

Available August 2000 at your favorite retail outlet.

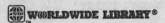

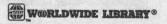

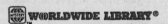

SIMON BRETT

Mrs. Pargeter's Point of Honour

A MRS. PARGETER MYSTERY

While activities of her dearly departed husband often took place beyond the confines of the law, the genteel Mrs. Pargeter considers it a point of honour to resolve any unfinished business he left behind.

Veronica Chastaigne, widow to one of Mr. Pargeter's partners in crime, is anxious to return her gallery of priceless "borrowed" paintings to their rightful owners. Graciously accommodating, Mrs. P. assembles her husband's cast of merry crooks to smuggle a fortune in Rembrandts and da Vincis out of England. But a caper worthy of dear Mr. P. wouldn't be up to snuff without the challenges of a bumbling inspector, a mysterious informant and a crafty interloper who manages to steal the paintings first....

Available September 2000
at your favorite retail outlet.

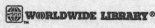 **WORLDWIDE LIBRARY®**

Visit us at www.worldwidemystery.com
WSB361

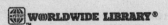